MW01681624

# *The* FALL OF FLETCHER CAMP NINE

## AN ELEVEN YEAR OLD GIRL MEETS A FLORIDA HURRICANE

CLIFTON WELSH

This is a work of fiction. Names, characters, places, and incidents are either the product of the author's imagination or are used fictitiously. Any resemblance to actual persons, living or dead, events, or locales is entirely coincidental.



First paperback edition September 2023
Contact the author at: CliftonWelsh33@gmail.com

Book design: Jack McNeil



ISBN: 978-1-7334601-7-0

# TABLE OF CONTENTS

1. Train Ride ........ 4
2. To Sebring ........ 9
3. Arrival at Laketon ........ 14
4. Laketon Hotel ........ 22
5. The Fortress ........ 28
6. Fletcher Camp Nine ........ 36
7. Lungraun' s Island ........ 42
8. New Quarters ........ 50
9. House Rule Number Four ........ 59
10. The King ........ 67
11. Fourth of July ........ 74
12. Fresh Dinner ........ 84
13. Skunked ........ 92
14. Missing Gator ........ 99
15. Lawrence Returns ........ 108
16. Departure for FC9 ........ 115
17. Unpleasant Discovery ........ 120
18. Ride to the Fortress ........ 130
19. Boat Crisis ........ 140
20. New Danger ........ 147
21. Broken Window ........ 153
22. Winning the Hoist ........ 160
23. Unexpected Finish ........ 167
24. End of Brightness ........ 178
25. Fall of the Fortress ........ 187
26. Tense Moment ........ 195
27. Fresh Start ........ 202
28. Rescue ........ 210
29. Debriefing ........ 219
30. Secret Plan ........ 230
31. Departure ........ 240
Epilogue ........ 248
Acknowledgements ........ 251

# CHAPTER 1

# TRAIN RIDE

*Dear Diary. Today is the 15th of June of 1927. This day ends my four-day trip from Canton, Ohio, to Laketon, Florida. Early this morning the train left Tampa and is supposed to arrive in Laketon by evening. That is, if the train makes it to Laketon. Such a small engine! It has only two big wheels on each side. Besides the tender loaded with coal and water, it pulls a mail car, a boxcar, an empty flatcar, and the single passenger coach where I sit.*

*The coach is old and worn. It has ten rows of seats (more like benches with hard leather surfaces) with an aisle down the middle. Lots of initials are carved into the exposed wood. If the car were full, it could seat forty people.*

Elsie Lungraun lowers her pen as she surveys the coach. She brushes away a curl of auburn brown hair that has slipped off her forehead and over one eye. Then she resumes writing.

*Today it carries only seven including me. Up near the front of the car sit four workmen - if the word 'sit' is a proper description. One is draped over the back of his seat like a soiled shawl. Another rests on his back with his legs at the knees hanging over the end of his seat and partially blocking the aisle. With unkempt hair dangling over his forehead down almost to his eyes, the largest man stands shirtless while talking toward the others. I can see his mouth moving and can barely hear sound, but I cannot make out what he is saying. I wonder if the others care. The fourth man seems disinterested as he sits looking out the window. They all seem to have dirty faces, but from where I sit I cannot tell whether their faces are unwashed or unshaven.*

*About five rows back a woman sits alone on the opposite side next to the window. She is kind of pretty. Dressed in a crisp white blouse and covered with a white hat lined with white feathers, she sits formally erect. Glowing white in the morning sun shining through her window, she seems so out of place on this train.*

*Finally, behind me on the last row across the aisle on the left side of the car sits the conductor. He is an older gentleman, but not too old, and has a round face with a pleasant smile. The sight of him in his fitted uniform contrasts with the four men at the front of the car. His cap really identifies him. He must be proud of being a conductor.*

Elsie turns several pages back in her diary and rereads her morning entry. Then closing the book she places it and her pen back into a small travel bag sitting next to her on the weathered leather seat and leans toward the open window. The tinge of coolness of the early morning has given way to comfortable warmth. White cotton-puff clouds populate what was once a cloudless tropical blue sky when the train departed Tampa.

Grass. Grass everywhere as far as the eye can see. Tall grass that could easily hide an eleven year old girl. Green grass interspersed with islands of trees. As she leans next to the window Elsie pushes the 'chug chug' of the locomotive along with the 'clickety-clack' of wheels crossing over rail joints and the squeaking of the coach as it rocks back and forth out of her mind. She pretends she is a gazelle running and jumping through the grass at the speed of the train.

*Wow! That was close!* Elsie's gazelle barely dodges a branch as the railroad cuts through an island of trees. The encounter startles her thoughts back to her seat. Shortly she notices a slowing of the rhythm from the rails. Risking an uncomfortable encounter with a piece of ash, a fly, or a bee, she leans out of the window to investigate. Ahead in the distance looms a large man-made structure standing very close to the tracks.

The brakes on all the cars squeal as the train slows. Then the brakes growl as the train grinds to a halt. All is silent.

"Ahem," sounds a man's voice from behind her.

Elsie pulls her head back into the car to face the conductor.

"The train is stopping to load up more coal and water," he smiles with a pleasant voice. He reaches into his pocket and retrieves a round silver pocket watch attached to a chain linked to his belt. Looking at his watch, he continues. "Looks like we are about on time."

The conductor drops his watch back into his pocket. "We should be arriving in Sebring in about an hour. It is best that you stay on the train. I will bring you some food and water."

"Thank you, sir."

The conductor departs and Elsie slides her head back outside of the window. A spout from a water tank on top of a wooden platform stretches over the tender. The fireman has climbed down from the locomotive and is shoveling coal from a pile stacked in a shed beneath the water tank into a large pail, which he hands up to the engineer.

But what strikes Elsie most is the silence. There are no birds singing or dogs barking. She is far enough back from the water tank not to hear the sounds the men are making. The grass bends limply in the calm. The comfortable warmth she felt in the breeze of the moving train is becoming uncomfortable heat in the windless spaces of the parked train.

Time seems to slow down. The heat is becoming oppressive.

CHAPTER 2

# TO SEBRING

'Twooot!' A single blast from the locomotive's whistle alerts all that the train is about to move. Elsie pulls back from the window and sits down, and not a moment too soon. 'Clank!' The coach jerks into motion.

'Chug, chug, chug!' As the train picks up speed, a breeze enters the window just as small beads of perspiration form on her forehead above her eyebrows.

'Clickety-clack, Clickety-clack!' Elsie looks out over the sea of grass interspersed with islands of trees. The gazelle has left her mind. The monotony of it all gradually settles over her. Now sitting restlessly in her seat, she searches for something different to occupy her time. There, just ahead on the other side of the aisle, sits the woman with the white feather-covered hat. It wouldn't hurt to talk with her.

She slides off her seat, walks up the aisle, and silently stands beside the women's bench. Eventually, the woman turns to look at her. Elsie smiles. "Hi. I'm Elsie Lungraun."

A smile spreads across the woman's face. Her voice is pleasant. "Hello, I'm Angela Diamond."

"Are you going to Laketon?"

"No, I get off at Sebring."

"Do you live in Sebring?"

"Sometimes. I will live there three weeks, maybe a month. Sometimes I live in Laketon, sometimes in Tampa."

"You own three houses?" queries Elsie with a raised voice.

"No, I stay at different houses."

"What do you do?"

Angela studies Elsie for a moment. "How old are you?"

"Eleven."

"Hmmm. My job is to help people feel better,"

replies Angela. Her voice is sweet and soothing and Elsie feels drawn to her.

"How do you make...?"

Angela cuts her off. "Elsie, do you live in Laketon?"

"No, I'm from Canton, Ohio. I am traveling to Laketon on my way to visit my cousin."

"Does your cousin live in Laketon?"

"No, the train stops in Laketon. The conductor told me that the railroad ends at Laketon. I will have to stay overnight in Laketon, and he will help me get on another train that goes to Fletcher Camp Nine."

The smile slowly dissolves from Angela's face. "You are going to Fletcher Camp Nine?"

"Have you been there?" queries Elsie with growing uncertainty.

Angela lifts her hand to her chin. "Yes, I have been there. Several times."

"Is Fletcher Camp Nine a pleasant town?"

"Fletcher Camp Nine isn't a town..." Angela pauses to carefully select her choice of words. "...er, it is a temporary town."

"What is that?"

"Well, a temporary town is a town that is not built

to last. The railroad is being extended from Laketon south through the Everglades to Miami. Fletcher Camp Nine is where the workers live. Once the railroad is finished the town will be torn down. So, Fletcher Camp Nine has no parks, no paved streets, and no running water, er, at least no good running water."

Elsie looks at Angela pensively. "Gee, that sounds awful."

"Since the buildings are all temporary, they are not well-built. Stairs are rickety; walls are drafty; roofs leak. It's hot in summer and cold in winter."

"Hmmm. Maybe that's why my cousin doesn't live there."

"Doesn't live there? Where does your cousin live?"

"On an island about two miles away."

Angela smiles again. "Hats off to your cousin."

"Well, perhaps to my uncle. He's my father's brother."

'Twoot! Twoot!'

"We are stopping outside of Sebring to switch onto a siding that will take us to the station," proclaims the conductor loudly as he walks up the aisle. "If you have baggage to claim, pick it up at the mail car. For now stay in your seats. Wait for the engine whistle that will signal when you can leave the car."

He stops at the seat where Elsie and Angela sit. "Miss Lungraun, please take your seat."

"Yes sir."

With the squeaking of brakes the train grinds to a stop. Silence. Elsie looks out of her window. Nothing but grass. She looks out the windows on the other side. A few distant buildings invade the grass.

'Clang, clang.' The faint distant sound is the only clue Elsie has that the train is moving again. She returns to her window. Only by studying the ground can she tell that the coach is moving. Slowly, very slowly.

'Clang, clang.' The sound draws closer. 'Clang, clang! Clang, clang!' The coach sways. Silence. Then a brief squeak of breaks as the train stops.

'Twooot.' After much fanfare, the four workmen hustle down the aisle and depart the train. Then Angela Diamond produces a large travel bag from beneath her seat and steps into the aisle. As she passes by Elsie she smiles. "Goodbye Elsie. Have a good trip."

Angela walks on and disappears.

CHAPTER 3

# ARRIVAL AT LAKETON

The passenger coach is beginning to heat up again. Fortunately, a cloud blocks the sun before the heat becomes unbearable. Elsie sits obediently in her seat listening for noises. Faint men's voices drift through the open windows on the opposite side of the coach. The voices grow louder, then are overcome by the grinding noise of the iron wheels of a loaded baggage wagon being pushed over a nearby cement walkway. As the sounds of men and wagon fade, Elsie sits in silence again.

"In about fifteen minutes," the conductor yells as he steps aboard the coach. He hands Elsie a bologna sandwich, an apple, and a canteen of water and departs the coach again. One bite of the sandwich tells her how hungry she is. She gobbles the sandwich and devours the apple. She looks around to see if anyone is watching. Finding that no one is, she tosses the apple core out the window next to her and sits back in the silence.

'Twoot! Toweeeet! A distant whistle draws Elsie's attention. In a few moments she can hear a locomotive approaching. 'Chug, chug, chug, CHUG, CHUG!' A gust of wind buffets her coach. She turns to her window just in time to watch the locomotive speed by. *One, two, three, four, five, six, seven, eight, nine, ten, eleven.* Elsie counts the cars as the freight train speeds past. Wow! she thinks to herself. Eleven cars! She listens as the roar of the freight train diminishes to a barely noticeable low rumble.

"All aboard!" shouts the conductor as he stands just outside by the steps up into the coach. The four workmen clamber back onboard, talking as if to no one as they return to their original seats at the front of the car. Then the conductor boards the train, closes the door, and takes his seat.

'Twooot!' 'Clank!' The car jerks into motion. 'Chug, chug!' The train moves slowly away from the Sebring station. 'Clang, clang!' 'Clang, clang!' The coach rocks as the train pulls off the siding and back onto the main line. 'Chug, chug, chug!' The train picks up speed. The buildings of Sebring disappear as Elsie reenters the sea of grass.

'Clickety-clack, Clickety-clack!' 'Squeak, squeak!' Elsie turns and looks back at the conductor. "Mister Conductor, may I please have a pillow?"

The conductor opens a small storage compartment, extracts a small white pillow, and brings it to Elsie. "There you are Miss Lungraun."

"Thank you."

Elsie places the pillow on her seat nearest the aisle. Then she lies on her back with her head on the pillow and her feet pressing against the side of the car below the open window. As she looks out, all she can see is sky and distant clouds. The whole picture seems fixed as the coach rattles and squeaks beneath her.

As she closes her eyes she lets her mind drift back to memories logged in her diary. Her adventure actually began two years ago when she was nine years old. Her uncle, Lawrence Lungraun, an employee of Steel Products Company of Canton, Ohio, approached his boss, Maxwell Lungraun, foundry supervisor, his brother and Elsie's father. He had an 'itch' to leave his job at Canton and move south. A railroad was building a line from Laketon, Florida, south across the Everglades toward Miami. The work was hard but the pay was good.

*Father was sad to see uncle Lawrence leave. He promised that, if things in Florida didn't work out, he could be sure his foundry job would be waiting for him when he returned to Canton. Our families are close and often share meals together. Lawrence's son, Tommy, is my age and we play all sorts of games during family visits.*

*So, when Uncle Lawrence and his family left for Florida, it left empty places in us all. Aunt Molly, Lawrence's wife, promised to write frequently, which she did. They arrived at Fletcher Camp Nine and Uncle Lawrence was assigned work on one of the track-laying crews. After six weeks he was put in charge of his work crew and then promoted several more times until he became supervisor for procurement.*

*Aunt Molly made it clear that Fletcher Camp Nine was not a place to raise children. So Uncle Lawrence bought an island about two miles from town and built a cabin large enough for four people. He bought a seventeen foot wooden boat propelled by a six horsepower Johnson motor and used it to haul all of the building materials to his island.*

*Then, about six months ago, came the real shocker. Uncle Lawrence and Aunt Molly invited me to spend two months of the summer at their island. Mother was immediately opposed to the idea. She didn't want me carted off to some wilderness where I could be lost. But Father thought it might be a good idea. After Uncle Lawrence and his family left Canton, I moped around trying to make new friends. Spending part of a summer in Florida among family might be good for me. Even educational!*

*Mother remained opposed to the idea. Then Father contacted the local railroad and found that special 'escorts' were assigned to care for and protect 'un-accompanied minors.' Mother's opposition gradually faded and so, here I am on this train to Laketon and on my way to Fletcher Camp Nine.*

Gradually the clickity-clack of wheels rolling over gaps in the rails and the squeaking of the rocking passenger coach fade away.

Elsie awakes while being shaken by the conductor. "Miss Lungraun, please get up. I have to close the window!"

She sits up, surprised by how dark it has become. Had she slept until dusk? "What time is it?" she asks the conductor.

"About four-o'clock," he replies as he closes the window. "We are approaching a bad storm."

The conductor walks on to close other windows. Elsie surveys the black sky. Angry clouds appear from over the train and fill the sky ahead as far as the eye can see. "Oh!" she exclaims as a brilliant bolt of lightning drops from a cloud to the ground and flashes several times. Another lightning bolt drops even closer. 'CRACK!'

Suddenly the roar of water falling on the roof of the coach drowns out all other sound. Sheets of rain slam against the window. More bright flashes of lightning! Elsie slides away from the window and sits near the aisle, staring straight ahead.

The tempest continues unabated for about a half an hour. Then the rain lessens and the skies become brighter. As the storm dies down she begins to notice that the train is slowing down. Finally it stops. She slides to the window expecting to see another coal and water station. There is nothing but grass.

'Twoot." The train slowly moves but it doesn't pick up speed. 'Clank, clank.' The coach rocks. 'Clank, clank.' The coach rocks again and squeaks. The train is pulling onto a siding. Elsie presses her cheek against the window to see what is happening. Its drive wheels turning slowly, the locomotive rounds a sharp curve ahead. 'Clank, clank.' 'Clank, clank.' The coach rocks again. Then it stops.

Elsie's eyes widen at the sight of shafts of sunlight streaming down as the early evening sun breaks through the storm clouds. She is looking to the west so that means the train has turned south.

'Twoot.' The car jolts unexpectedly backward. *This train is backing up!*

All she can see is grass. Then a shanty facing the tracks drifts slowly by. A second shanty. A building with a large overhang and men working among some machinery. A street lined with houses and white picket fences. The back of a two-story brick and stucco building. Then a street lined with cars and a row of storefronts facing the tracks. It appears the train is backing into a sort of town square.

The train slows to a halt. 'Twoot, twoot!" The conductor steps into the aisle. "Okay folks, we have arrived at Laketon. This is the end of the line. Everyone must leave this car."

He then turns to Elsie. "Miss Lungraun, please remain in your seat. I will return to escort you to your hotel."

"Thank you."

# CHAPTER 4

# LAKETON HOTEL

The four workmen stampede from their places in the front of the coach, past Elsie, and almost overrun the conductor, who hastens out of their way. They disappear out of the coach and momentarily their voices fade into the distance.

With the coach now empty and quiet, Elsie slips to a seat on the opposite side. Just below her next to the steps that enter the car stands the conductor. Beyond him is a cement walkway for passengers and baggage carts. Beyond that is a green area populated with palm trees. Then a street. And beyond the street stands an elegant white stucco two-story building with a colonnaded carriage shelter over an arched front door. Above the front door she can make out the words 'Laketon Hotel.'

"Well, Bob. About time," huffs the annoyed conductor.

"Sorry it took so long but we had to work through a mix-up in luggage. Here is your special delivery."

The man hands a piece of luggage to the conductor. Elsie recognizes the suitcase as hers.

"Miss Lungraun," calls the conductor as he leans toward the entrance to the car. "You may come out now and I will take you to your hotel."

Elsie scrambles from her seat and appears at the top of the stairs. As she climbs down, the conductor guides her step to the pavement. Then, carrying her suitcase, he escorts her across the street to the hotel, opens the door, and holds it for her to enter. Once inside, they enter the dining room.

The hostess smiles from behind her desk. "Good evening; how can I help you?"

The conductor produces a letter, surveys its lines and replies. "Is Missus Wilson in?"

"She is. Whom shall I say is calling?"

"I am the conductor of the Tampa to Laketon train

and I am escorting Miss Elsie Lungraun to this hotel for the night."

"Oh, yes. Please sit in the dining room while I locate Missus Wilson."

The hostess vanishes while Elsie and the conductor step into the dining room. Elsie's eyes widen. Everything looks so new. Stained wooden chairs sit before stained wooden tables. Along one wall runs a padded leather bench above which rises a large mural showing water, grass, and trees against a brilliant blue sky.

An attractive young woman in a flowing flowered dress walks up to them and turns to the conductor. "I am Betsy Wilson and this must be Elsie."

"Yes, Ma'am. I am conductor of the Tampa to Laketon train and my instructions are to place Miss Lungraun into your care."

The conductor turns to Elsie and finishes. "I have to say, 'farewell.' You will need to be up for breakfast by seven-thirty tomorrow. My train returns to Tampa at eight. Then your train to Fletcher Camp Nine should depart at nine."

He tips his hat to Elsie and then to Betsy Wilson.

"Good evening."

The conductor departs. Betsy smiles at Elsie. "You must be hungry. We have dinner prepared for you but first let's see Edward at the reservation desk and find which room you will be staying in tonight."

Betsy marches Elsie toward a dapper gentleman standing behind the reservation counter. "Edward. This is Elsie Lungraun. The railroad has posted a reservation for her tonight."

The man looks down at his books. "Yes, Miss Lungraun. I have a place for you in Room 5. It has a separate bathroom."

He turns to the room key box behind him, extracts the key from the space under the number '5,' and hands the key to Betsy. As she turns to escort Elsie to her room, she sees a porter standing nearby. "John, go to the dining room and bring the brown suitcase to me at Room 5."

The porter turns toward the dining room. Meanwhile Betsy leads Elsie down the hall to the door with the number '5.' She inserts the key into the door lock and the door swings open. Elsie is delighted by what she sees. The walls are adorned with light-blue flowered wallpaper. Against one wall sits a stained-oak dresser. Next to it stands a wardrobe of identical construction. Protruding into the room near the opposite wall is the largest bed she has ever seen. It sits high off the floor, so high in fact that she might have to stand on a chair to climb into it. Four oak pillars rise from the corners of the bed to support a canopy above it.

Elsie pulls back the light blue pastel curtains. The window overlooks the front of the hotel. In the rapidly dwindling evening twilight the Tampa train is barely visible in the darkening shadows. Turning to Betsy, Elsie exclaims, "This is a beautiful room. I love it!"

"Wonderful!" replies Betsy. "Why don't we return to the dining room for your dinner? You must be hungry after such a long trip."

Betsy guides Elsie to her table. Several other people are also dining but Elsie is too tired and hungry to notice much about them. The waitress appears carrying a large plate with slices of roast beef, mashed potatoes, and peas, all of which are covered in warm brown gravy. While trying to look ladylike, Elsie devours her meal. All that remains is to do something about her fatigue.

She waves to the waitress and tells her that she would like to return to her room. Betsy escorts her to her room and reminds her to lock the door from the inside. "Good night, Elsie. I will have someone wake you at seven-thirty."

Elsie washes from her face some of the humidity acquired during the day, brushes her teeth, and puts on her pajamas. She slides a chair next to the bed and climbs up to the soft mattress. She turns out the lights, pulls the covers up to her chin, and that is all she remembers.

## CHAPTER 5

# THE FORTRESS

'Knock, knock, knock!' 'Knock, knock, knock!'
"Miss Lungraun? Elsie Lungraun?"

"Yes."

"It's seven-thirty!"

"Thank you."

Elsie rises and looks out of her window. The Tampa train is gone. As she washes and prepares for breakfast, a feeling of excitement blossoms within. Today is the day she sees Tommy and his parents, Lawrence and Molly. Today is the day her long journey ends. She opens her suitcase and withdraws a clean pair of blue denim shorts. Then she adds a bright yellow blouse.

After departing her room and locking the door, she appears in the dining room. It is full of people, but one table has been reserved for her. Shortly after she takes her seat the waitress appears with a glass of juice and two plates, one with a scrambled egg and two strips of bacon and the other with two buttermilk pancakes. As she sets the plates before Elsie she smiles. "Here is fresh-squeezed orange juice and plenty of food. Eat up, Dearie. It's a long way to Fletcher Camp Nine."

As Elsie enjoys her breakfast, she notices more customers leaving their tables and departing the dining room. Motion from outside captures her attention. A train is slowly backing into place across the street. She can clearly see the passenger coach, three box cars and part of the mail car. A crowd is beginning to gather along the cement walkway.

Anxiety flutters through Elsie's heart. She is barely halfway through her breakfast. But wait! The conductor told her that the train would return to Tampa at eight o'clock. Its a few minutes before eight. There he is! The conductor! It is the Tampa train. Elsie's train has not yet arrived. Whew!

Elsie relaxes as she finishes her breakfast. Then she

returns to her room, brushes her teeth, and repacks her belongings into her suitcase. She departs her room, locks the door, and places the key on the reservation desk. As she carries her suitcase toward the dining room she is met by Betsy Wilson. "Good morning, Miss Lungraun. Are you ready to board your next train?"

"Yes, Ma'am."

"Why don't you sit on the bench just outside the hotel door? You can watch for your train to arrive."

Betsy escorts Elsie to a bench just outside the front door of the hotel. She sits in the shade of the building in the cool of the morning, if a morning in the mid-June humidity of south Florida can be considered cool. The fronts of the buildings across the street glow in the heat of direct sunlight.

It's eight-thirty. A train backs slowly up the track in front of the hotel where Elsie sits. There is a passenger coach much like the one that transported her from Tampa to Laketon. Then there is the empty flat car and a box car. Except for a little more rust, the locomotive is almost identical to the one that pulled the Tampa train.

The train stops. Three men depart the passenger car and disappear down the cement walk. A fourth man, dressed in jeans and a tattered white T-shirt, disembarks the car and approaches the hotel. He seems to be carrying what looks like a conductor's cap. He passes by Elsie and enters the hotel.

Twenty minutes later the man reemerges from the hotel as he wipes his lips with the back of his right hand. Betsy Wilson is behind him. They stop in front of Elsie. Betsy speaks. "Miss Lungraun, this is Mike. He is the conductor on the train to Fletcher Camp Nine. He will be your escort there."

Elsie studies the man facing her. He looks unkempt, almost seedy, and can't be older than eighteen. She is instantly uneasy.

Mike smiles at her as he puts on his conductor's hat. "Welcome aboard the best train in south Florida, Miss Lungraun. By the way, I have a message from your uncle. You are to remain at the FC9 station until his family can meet you there."

Elsie's uneasiness dissolves.

Mike bends down slightly to grasp Elsie's suitcase. "Come, Miss Lungraun. It's time to board the train."

"Goodbye," calls Betsy as Mike and Elsie approach the street.

The four workmen who had been on the Tampa train stand at the bottom of the steps into the passenger car. Two more join them. Mike and Elsie approach the men. "Step aside, meatheads," cajoles Mike. "Make way for a real lady."

"Where's your monkey suit," replies one contemptuously.

"Train's not ready to board. Only VIPs allowed," replies Mike as he guides Elsie past them. He pauses for her to climb the steps ahead of him. Then he follows her onboard. "Any seat in the last three rows is reserved for you."

"I know where to sit," Elsie replies as she settles onto a bench on the right-hand side of the car.

"Very good. I will place your suitcase on the bench behind you. By the way, Miss Lungraun, do you have a first name?"

"Elsie."

"May I address you by your first name?"

"Yes. May I address you as 'Mike'?"

"Fair enough."

Mike turns back to the stairs and calls down, "All aboard!"

The six workmen clamber up the stairs and tussle among themselves to see who is first to the front of the car. They take no notice of Elsie.

After a few minutes Elsie notices movement outside. The storefronts across the town square are moving slowly past her. The train started so slowly that she didn't notice. The back of a two-story brick and stucco building glides past, then a street lined with houses and white picket fences, then a building with a large overhanging roof below which are workers surrounding some machines, then several shanties, and then grass. Laketon is left behind.

Elsie quickly grows bored with the view outside and settles into filling her diary with the day's information. After several hours she looks out again. Still grass everywhere. Grass waving in the breeze. But there is one difference. Running alongside the train is a canal about fifty feet wide.

An opportunity presents itself as Conductor Mike goes to the front of the car to quiet the raucous crowd there. As he returns Elsie questions, "Mike, why is there a canal along the tracks?"

"We are riding on all-new rail. To build the roadbed we dredged up surrounding rock and that created the canal."

"I saw an animal swimming in the canal. Do you know…?"

Mike cuts her off. "Probably an alligator. There are lots of them around here in the canals."

"What is an alligator?"

"An ugly, nasty critter. Really mean. You don't want to mess with them."

Mike walks on. Elsie turns back to the window and surveys the canal. *Hmmm. I wonder if I can see any more alligators.*

It must be about noon, judging from the shadows cast by the grass, when Elsie makes a new discovery. The light from the sky reflecting off the water of the canal seems to be surrounding the grass. Yes, the grass is standing in water!

Now and then side channels appear giving Elsie a deeper view into the grassy sea. Some channels widen, occasionally revealing ponds and small lakes. Now the grassy scene is passing by more slowly. Elsie perceives that the train is slowing down.

The grass gives way to a huge lake or bay with a few small islands but mostly water all the way to the horizon. The train continues on slowly. Then it stops. Elsie sticks her head out of the window for a better view. The wall of grass from whence they have come is barely visible behind them. As she looks forward, all she can see is more water. The sun is beginning to shine through her window so she leaves her seat for the seat across the aisle. The view from there is the same.

After about half an hour the train proceeds slowly. Massive iron I-beams rising up to form a long truss bridge pass slowly by. After the train crosses the bridge, a large cement structure looms into view. About thirty feet long and twenty feet high, it is entered by a small door built into a larger sliding door made of vertically hung wooden clapboards. Several men stand in front of the structure.

The train stops again. Mike's voice from behind startles her. "That's a machine and engine fitting and repair shop. The walls are sixteen inches thick. Solid poured cement. Has all sorts of hoists and pulleys for lifting heavy stuff. We call it 'the fortress'."

CHAPTER 6

# FLETCHER CAMP NINE

Conductor Mike steps to the back to open the door, giving entry to the coach. Workmen climb aboard and begin filling the seats. Elsie counts fifteen new passengers bringing the total number of workmen onboard to twenty-one.

She moves back to her original seat, which is now drenched in light from the early afternoon sun. Sunlight also sparkles on little wavelets kicked up by a light breeze.

The train is moving again yet not very fast. 'Clang, clang.' 'Clang, clang.' The coach rocks and Elsie senses that the train is going around a sharp curve. The invasion of sunlight through her window draws back then disappears, leaving her sitting in the shade. 'Clang, clang.' 'Clang, clang.' 'Chug, chug.' The train picks up speed.

The water looks like glass. Blue sky and white puffy clouds reflect almost perfectly. A stand of flooded grass passes by. Then more grass pushes open water to the distance. In a moment the grass is gone and the water is back. After a few minutes, stands of grass reappear. Again, open water is pushed to the distance, then out of sight. A mangrove tree passes by. More grass then more mangrove trees.

'Twoot!' 'Twoot!' 'Twoot, twoot.' 'Twooot!' The train is slowing down. A cluster of small wooden shacks drifts into view. Their distinguishing characteristic is that all share slightly rusted corrugated tin roofs. Next there appears a field filled with tents ordered in rows. More wooden structures appear. All are unpainted and weathered. The largest building is a two-story box clad with overlapping wooden siding. The word, 'HOTEL' is stamped on the side facing the railroad.

Conductor Mike steps up the aisle. "Alright everyone. We are approaching the FC9 station. Make sure everything you brought on leaves with you. I am not your mother."

Then he turns toward Elsie. "Elsie, please remain seated until everyone else has departed the car."

"Yes sir."

The coach's wheels squeal as the train comes to a halt at the FC9 station, a weathered wooden building with a corrugated tin roof much like the others Elsie had seen as they approached. The workmen stand and file out of the car. She watches them scatter across the raised wooden plank platform, which looks long enough to service two coaches.

Elsie takes the opportunity to slide to a window on the opposite side of the car. Her coach sits at the edge of a small switch yard of maybe six sidings. There are scattered box cars, some with doors closed and others with doors slid open. Two flat cars hold pieces of machinery. Further away sits a string of flat cars loaded with rail and ties. Finally, at the far side of the switch yard, sits a locomotive much like the one that had pulled her train. There is no smoke or steam; it is just sitting there.

Beyond the switch yard a line of wooden structures with corrugated tin roofs gives the impression of some sort of industry. To the far right at the end of the tracks stand a water tower and a wooden tank, elevated by a wooden platform, that looks much like the coal and water station the Tampa train stopped at before arriving at Sebring.

After all the workmen have disembarked Mike returns and approaches Elsie. "Elsie, let's move you to the station. I have found a secure place where you can sit until someone from your uncle's family comes by to get you."

Elsie follows Mike, who carries her piece of luggage, from the coach, across the wooden platform and through a door into the station. They pass by the ticket-teller's window and into a small empty waiting room lined with enough benches to seat perhaps twenty. Sunlight coming through a clerestory on the south-facing wall illuminates the room.

Elsie follows Mike as he turns along this wall to the door of a small office. He leads her into the office, which is empty except for a small table and two chairs. Placing her suitcase at the foot of the table he turns and smiles. "The station-master and the ticket-taker know that you are here and will direct your family to this office when they arrive. Make yourself comfortable."

Mike departs the office, closing the door behind him. Elsie looks around the room. The door has a small square window at eye level which allows one to see out into the waiting room. A larger window at the back of the room views out over the station platform toward the switch yard. The train crew must have uncoupled the coach because it sits by itself along the platform in clear view.

On one wall hangs a large map showing a black line drawn from Laketon to Miami. About half-way along the line, another line runs from it at a near right angle to a small island below which is written the letters 'FC9.' The part of the line from Laketon to maybe a quarter of the way past the FC9 cutoff toward Miami is wider than the rest of the line. Elsie ponders whether the thicker line represents that part of the railroad which has been completed.

Voices in the waiting room draw Elsie's attention away from the map. Elsie can barely hear a woman's voice questioning a man. "Should be in the office," he replies as his voice grows louder.

"Is she here? Is she here, Mommy?" calls Tommy's

voice.

"We will see," she replies.

Elsie looks toward the door. However, instead of approaching the door, she shrinks back toward the table. The knob turns and the door opens. There, standing before her, are Aunt Molly Lungraun and Cousin Tommy. Tommy jumps up and down. "Yippee, she's here; she's here!"

Molly steps forward and wraps Elsie in a tight hug. "Elsie, Elsie! Let's don't be shy, shall we? Welcome to Florida."

CHAPTER 7

# LUNGRAUN'S ISLAND

Molly coaxes Elsie toward the door. Tommy is still jumping. "Yippee, she's here; she's here!"

Elsie slowly approaches her hopping cousin. Then she breaks out in a broad grin and starts jumping with him. Molly stands erect, folds her arms across her chest and relaxes.

"Wow! I've got lots of things to show you! We are going to have fun!" exclaims Tommy, as he gains control of his emotions.

"All well and good!" replies Molly with a slightly scolding tone. "But first we have some errands to complete, don't we?"

Tommy's enthusiasm drains away as he stares at his mother. Now that she has the attention of both children, Molly proclaims, "We are here not just to gather up Elsie; we are here to gather up supplies for a week. We have an additional mouth to feed. So, let's be off to the grocery."

She steps around the children with an unspoken command to follow her and proceeds across the waiting room toward the front door of the railroad station. Understanding Molly's body language, the two follow her through the door, down a wooden step, and onto a broad sandy street. Here and there a few small patches of grass struggle against trampling by feet and crushing by wheels.

Molly leads her crew across the street toward another nondescript wooden structure topped with a corrugated tin roof. Its identifying feature is the word 'Grocery' stamped in large weathered letters barely visible above the door.

Once inside Elsie looks up at a row of skylights running the full length of the building. Rows of shelves stocked with foodstuffs sit bathing in the bright afternoon sun. "Get me one of those shopping carts," Molly commands Tommy. After a short while the shopping cart is filling up. Much to Tommy's and Elsie's delight, some of the load has come from the cookie and chocolate aisle.

By using an adding machine with a hand crank, the store manager totals their bill and checks them out. Their load of groceries fills two cardboard boxes. As Molly makes payment, she casually informs the manager that she will need help in transporting the boxes to the local dock. The manager turns toward the back of the store and shouts, "LaRoy! LaRoy, bring up the wheelbarrow!"

Ten minutes later Molly and the two children arrive at Sutton's Dock and Marine Supply followed by a young man pushing a wheelbarrow loaded with boxes of groceries. Sutton's Dock is in a small harbor cut back into the sand of the island to form three sides of a box. A sand bar protects about two-thirds of the fourth side with the rest being a channel cut out into open water.

As one looks into the harbor from the channel, the building, equipped with a hoist for lifting boats from the water, sits on the far left side of the harbor. Wooden plank docks hug the other two sides. Two small boats are tied up along the longest dock which faces the main channel. The shortest dock, which extends from the end of the long dock almost to open water, faces Sutton's building. A somewhat larger boat equipped with an outboard motor is moored here. Molly leads her group toward the short dock.

Lawrence is waiting. He quickly unloads the wheelbarrow and sets the boxes on the dock. Then he gives a fifty-cent tip to the blond wavy-haired man with a boyish face and a facial expression of one who would rather be at the beach.

As LaRoy departs with the wheelbarrow, Lawrence turns his attention to Elsie. With a broad smile he steps toward her with hand extended. Elsie takes his hand. "Welcome to Florida," he begins as he shakes Elsie's hand. "I hope your trip was easy and there were no problems with the trains."

"No. Lot's of people watched after me and treated me very well."

"Good. Well…." He sweeps his arm in a half circle. "This is FC9. You've seen just about all of it. All of it that's worth seeing that is."

Then he sweeps his arm toward the wooden boat tied up at the dock. "Good-bye FC9. You are about to become a special guest at Lungraun's Island."

He turns and, using his foot, slides the boxes of groceries along the dock closer to his boat. "Looks like plenty of food for us for a few days."

"You got the other supplies?" queries Molly.

"Gas for the boat, fuel for the lamps, ten gallons of water in four canteens, a bag of coal for the stove, and feed for the chickens."

Molly smiles in approval as Lawrence steps down into the boat and steadies it next to the dock. Then he moves the boxes of groceries onto the hull between the second and third seats. Pointing to the seat at the bow he commands, "Molly, you get the front seat. Elsie, you sit on the second seat. Tommy gets the third seat and I sit in the back by the motor to run things."

Each person takes his/her assigned place. Tommy and Elsie carefully step over an oar lying across the seat but secured to the side. "Oh, dear!" exclaims Molly. "I forgot! We have left Elsie's suitcase at the train station."

Lawrence turns to Tommy. "Tommy, run fast to

the station and bring back Elsie's suitcase."

Tommy scrambles out of the boat and disappears down the dock. Meanwhile, Lawrence lifts a key attached to a small chain from around his neck, inserts the key into a lock embedded into the motor casing and gives it a quarter turn to the right. Grasping a handle at the top of the motor, he gives it a pull.

'Pop!' 'Pop!' 'Put, put, put.' 'Varooom!' Lawrence turns the motor's steering handle to reduce its speed to idle. Then they wait. After a few minutes Tommy reappears with Elsie's suitcase in hand. He lowers the suitcase down to Elsie and clambers aboard. "Okay," says Lawrence as he nods toward Tommy.

Tommy unties a rope securing the boat to a mooring post. Then Lawrence releases a rope around a similar post next to his seat. He pushes against the post, setting the boat free from the dock. Shifting the motor into reverse gear, Lawrence backs up the boat on a tight turn so that it comes to the middle of the harbor facing open water.

He shifts the motor into forward and they all feel the acceleration as the boat speeds from the harbor. Traveling several hundred feet out from the harbor, they turn away from the sun in an easterly direction running parallel to Fletcher Island. Elsie sees the grass of the distant shoreline turn in front of them. Lawrence calls forward to Elsie to give her a perspective on where they are headed. "We call this 'Bigger's Cove.' It protects Sutton's harbor from strong east winds. Sometimes we get sea breezes that come through from the east or southeast and the main channel gets rough. Bigger's cove makes it easy to get to the docks."

He changes course to take them directly away from the island. The early evening sun is hidden behind some distant clouds to the west. Lawrence continues his role as tour guide. "This is the main channel. It has some deep places but most of it is shallow. Not more than six feet deep in most places."

As they approach the grass lining the far side of the channel, Elsie notices a side channel opening up. They are headed straight into it.

"This side channel takes us another mile or more to our cabin," proclaims Lawrence.

A few turns through the side channel and the grass gives way enough to expose a man-made structure in the distance. As they get closer a dock appears.

Lawrence deftly guides the boat at full throttle toward the dock and, at just the right moment, cuts the motor and steers to a gliding stop, perfectly at a mooring pole. Tommy ties a rope to the pole while Lawrence secures the back of the boat to another one. They absorb the silence for a few moments and then Lawrence proclaims. "Welcome to Lungraun's Island."

CHAPTER 8

# NEW QUARTERS

By the time the boat is unloaded and supplies packed in their proper places it is almost dark. Lawrence departs for one his favorite pastimes – sitting on a bench at the end of the dock, smoking his pipe and watching the fading colors of sunset diminish from the clouds.

Meanwhile, Molly prepares an evening snack for Elsie and Tommy, an offering that is greatly appreciated. As they are finishing their meal, Lawrence returns and takes a chair next to the kitchen table. "Welcome, Elsie. How are your Mom and Dad?"

"Doing well when I left. Mom had finally agreed to my making this trip but she was sad to see me go.

I think both Mom and Dad really miss you. Dad said to tell you that you can have your job back should you return to Canton."

"Well, I instructed the ticket-master back at the station to telegraph Canton that you had arrived safely. Your folks should know that by now."

"How was your trip?" interrupts Molly.

"Aside from its being long, I met a lot of friendly people."

"Did the conductors take care of you? Were you left alone?"

"It seemed like the conductors were watching me all the time. When they weren't watching me, they made sure I was in the company of someone else. Someone they approved of, I guess. A conductor always made sure that I was secure in my sleeping compartment and a conductor always made sure I was at breakfast on time."

"You met a lot of friendly people?"

"Yes, very friendly. Treated me like a big person. Told me lots of stories of their travels. Places where they had been."

"Well, good! It seems like you had a…."

"Oh!" interrupts Elsie. "I met a really nice lady on the train to Laketon. She got off at Sebring. She knows about Fletcher Camp Nine. Said she had been here several times."

Both Lawrence and Molly give Elsie their full attention. "Do you remember who she was?" queries Molly.

"Hmmm. Let me think. Yes! Angela Diamond."

Molly glances toward Lawrence, who returns a small smile. "I have heard of her," replies Lawrence. "I have never met her but some of the workmen speak highly of her."

Molly and Lawrence go silent. Then Tommy turns to Elsie. "Want to see your room?"

The two, followed by Molly, head off to what is to be Elsie's room during her stay. It has one small dresser and a small bed. It is the bed that draws Elsie's attention. Its single mattress rests on a wooden platform with four poles positioned at the corners to support a canopy. The canopy looks less like a lacy fabric and more like a waterproof tarp. Over that is hung mosquito netting.

As Elsie surveys the room she notices white circles

that seem to be drawn randomly on the floor. "What are the white circles for?" she inquires.

Molly explains. "The roof leaks. When it rains, we put out pots and pans where we know the water comes in. Then, when the rain stops, we pick them up, pour them out, and wait for the next rain. But at least you won't get wet while sleeping. The canopy is waterproof and, as you can see, is hung so that the lowest part is midway along the foot of the bed. Any water that falls on it just drains off onto the floor.

Elsie looks toward a small double-hung window beside the bed. Its curtain is also mosquito netting. "Do you have lots of mosquitoes?"

"A few," replies Molly. "Kinda seasonal. There's a lot of shallow standing water around here. It's an ideal mosquito breeding area. However, we are fortunate to have a small fish, a minnow, that's a voracious eater of mosquito larvae. They keep the mosquito population down, but never completely."

The next morning the brilliance of the sun shining through the window next to her bed finally overcomes Elsie's instincts to catch up on sleep lost on trains and strange beds. She drags herself out of bed, puts on her day clothes, and exits her room for the kitchen.

As soon as she sits down at the kitchen table Molly places a small glass of freshly squeezed orange juice in front of her. "Good morning, Elsie. Did you sleep well last night?"

"Very well, thank you. I don't remember anything from the moment my head hit the pillow until waking up this morning."

Several pieces of raw bacon sizzle in a pan when Molly places it on the stove. She turns and calls toward an adjacent room. "Tommy, please find us some eggs for breakfast."

Tommy whizzes by and out the kitchen door. Molly begins to assemble pancake mix. In a few minutes Tommy returns with six eggs. "Wonderful!" exclaims Molly. "That's just what I need."

As preparations for breakfast grade into an actual breakfast, Lawrence appears to complete the group sitting around the kitchen table. Toward the end of the meal, Lawrence gains Tommy's attention. "Tommy, after breakfast I want you to give Elsie the 'house rules'."

Tommy nods.

As breakfast winds down, Lawrence dismisses himself to retreat to his bedroom to read. Molly collects dirty dishes and piles them to be washed. Tommy points to Elsie and, with his best impersonation of a parental voice, commands. “Come on. I have to show you the ‘house rules’.”

Without a word Elsie follows Tommy out the front door and onto the dock. He leads her to the far end where Lawrence has his ‘smoking’ bench. When she catches up with him and stands beside him, looking into the water at the end of the dock, Tommy proclaims. “The water here is three feet deep. As you can see, it is so clear that it doesn’t look like there is water here. The bottom is covered in white sand; there are a few shells and tuffs of grass growing on the bottom. It looks completely safe….” He pauses for effect, “…for now.”

“What do you mean?

“Every now and then things swim by, things that have teeth. So, rule number one: Never swim alone. If you want to go for a swim, get me or Mom to go with you. If you can’t get me or Mom to go with you, then don’t go swimming.”

Tommy turns to face the bench. "Rule number two: Don't sit on the dock with your feet dangling in the water, especially at night. If you want to sit on the dock, sit on the bench. That is the real reason why Dad put it out here."

"Why?"

"Same reason as for rule number one. Things that have teeth like to swim by at night. Come on. Let's go out back."

They walk back off the dock, go through the front door, through the kitchen, and out the back door. "Here's the chicken coupe where I went to get eggs this morning."

Tommy grasps a wooden pole of about six feet in length from where it leans against the chicken coop. Then Elsie follows him as he leads along a barely visible path. "This is a garden Dad keeps. Tomatoes, beans, beets, and a bunch of other stuff."

He walks beyond the garden for about fifty feet, stops, and waits for Elsie to stand beside him. "Lungraun's Island is supposed to be a mile long and a half-mile wide. However, that is only if large expanses of grass growing in shallow water are added in. The grass grows to three feet. That comes up almost to your arm pits. And there are places you might wander into that will make you a lot shorter."

Tommy pushes the pole into the submerged sand just ahead of his feet. Elsie's eyes widen and her jaw drops as the pole goes down and down, maybe two feet. "That's quicksand!"

Tommy continues. "That's what you call it. If you sink this far in this place you will be below the tops of the grass. No one can see you and that brings me to rule number three. 'Never wander away by yourself.'"

He pulls the pole from the sand. "Come on; let's go back to the house. I have a special thing to show you for rule number four."

As they walk back, Elsie queries, "Are there any snakes?"

"You afraid of snakes?"

"Yes. Isn't everyone?"

"Let's just say we treat snakes with caution. When we first moved here there were some rattlesnakes. Some coral snakes. Others that are non-poisonous. Don't know where they came from because we are on an island. Dad figures snakes swim in the water until they find land. Another good reason to follow house rules. Anyway Dad brought in a different kind of snake. Snakes that don't like snakes. Now we don't have much of a problem with snakes or other varmints that find their way onto the island."

CHAPTER 9

# HOUSE RULE NUMBER FOUR

They arrive back at the chicken coop, where Tommy leans his pole to the side. He produces a small pocket knife and cuts about a fifteen inch piece of heavy twine from a large spool spindled at the side of the coop. Handing the piece of twine to Elsie he speaks. “Here. Hold this.”

He then pulls off a much longer length of twine, about 50 feet, by walking it back to the garden. He cuts this string and then pulls off a new and an even longer length, about 100 feet, and cuts it off. He carefully loops each piece and swaps them for the fifteen inch piece Elsie holds.

Then he opens the coop and grabs a chicken by its

legs. 'Squawk, squawk.' "This old hen is almost past laying. She'll do."

Elsie looks on with alarm. "What are you doing?"

Tommy doesn't answer. He ties the hen's feet with the twine. Holding the chicken under his left arm and grasping his wooden pole he commences to walk in a new direction. "Follow me!"

Their new path runs parallel to the channel that runs past the dock. Using his pole, Tommy carefully prods his way through the stands of grass toward a distant mangrove tree. As they draw closer, the mangrove tree expands into several mangrove trees spaced along the edge of land.

They reach a space between two of the mangroves and stop. Elsie surveys the surroundings. The grass is shorter here. The mangroves offer some shade, a commodity otherwise absent on Lungraun's Island. And just offshore is a patch of lily pads which float as silent and motionless sentinels on the placid channel that perfectly reflects the blue of the sky and the white of scattered clouds. Its serenity is intoxicating.

"Over here," beckons Tommy as he steps toward a tall spindly tree.

"What kind of tree is that?" asks a cautious but curious Elsie.

The trunk of the tree is about ten inches in diameter at the ground. Its bark is smooth all the way up to a small 'bush' of leaves at the top – about 30 feet. "I don't know. I call it a 'cap tree' because the bunch of leaves at the top looks like someone wearing a cap."

"Strange. There are several of these trees here."

Tommy puts the chicken on the ground. "She won't be going anywhere with her legs tied."

Then he grasps the tree, pulls himself up, and wraps his legs around the trunk. "Watch this."

As he shinnies up the tree, it bends over slightly toward his weight. The higher he climbs the more the tree bends. Elsie giggles when Tommy finds himself 'climbing' horizontally. Then she laughs to see him shinnying down as the top of the tree now rests on the ground.

Now hanging upside down Tommy directs, "Elsie, tie one end of the shorter line of twine right here just below the bush of leaves."

Elsie does.

"Make sure it is tied tight."

"Okay. It's done."

Tommy lets go and falls to the ground. 'SWISH!' The tree springs back up taking the line of twine with it. Tommy picks up the free end of the twine and lays it down toward a second cap tree about 30 feet away. Then he beckons to Elsie. "Hand me the end of the long piece."

He ties the end into a loop, threads the free end of the first piece of twine through it, and places it on the ground. Then he climbs the second tree, bending it to the ground toward the first tree.

When the top of the tree touches the ground Tommy commands, "Tie the free end of the first piece to the top of this tree."

Elsie does. As Tommy lets go and drops to the ground, 'SWISH!' The tree springs back.

"What are you doing?" queries Elsie.

"Building a slingshot." He picks up the chicken, hands it to Elsie, and starts walking toward deeper grass away from the water. "Follow me."

Picking his way with the wooden pole in his right hand and unwinding the loop of twine held in his left hand, he reaches the end of the twine and stops.

"Here. Hold the chicken with its legs out."

Elsie does. Tommy ties the twine to the chicken's already bound legs. Then he grabs the twine and they both step farther into the grass, away from the water, pulling the tops of the cap trees toward them. Tommy stops and commands. "You stay here. I'm going to have to step a little toward the trees where I can pull harder to get the trees to bend down more so I can get more 'spring'."

He steps forward to a position where he can pull the trees downward giving more 'spring' to his slingshot. As he does, the length of line to Elsie slackens. Tommy calls back to Elsie. "Step backward to tighten up the line."

"NO! Absolutely not! I am NOT taking a single step back into this swamp!"

Tommy hangs his head, takes a deep breath, and exhales with a sigh as he collects his thoughts. He slowly releases the cap trees, picks up his wooden pole and walks back to Elsie. "Okay. Look! I am probing the ground all the way back to here! No water! No swamp! No snakes!"

He walks past Elsie without looking at her, grabs

the twine and pulls the trees toward him. "Okay, take a few steps back to tighten the line."

Elsie does.

Tommy pulls the trees down further. "Take a few more steps back."

Elsie does.

Finally he has pulled the trees down as far as he can without snapping the twine. "Okay. Don't squeeze the chicken. Hold it lightly with legs forward."

"Okay."

Tommy releases the trees. 'Swoosh!'

The chicken slips from Elsie's hands and files through the air.

'Squawk!' 'Squawk, squawk, squawk!'

While Elsie breaks into a run toward Tommy, he looks up with satisfaction to see that the chicken has catapulted about 50 feet overhead toward the water. She arrives at his side just in time to watch the bird, squawking and flapping its wings to brake its fall, settle in the water just beyond the lily pads.

Almost instantly the water boils next to the lily pads about 20 feet away. "Eeeek!" Elsie pushes her hands to the sides of her face in terror as two massive jaws protrude from the water and close on the chicken. The jaws and chicken disappear under the water, but the twine is still attached. The monster turns with full force, splashing water with its tail and jerking the cap trees overhead. With her hands still pressed against her face, Elsie shrinks back and doubles over slightly as if to shield her body from what she sees. The monster is at least ten feet long, maybe more! She screams!

'Snap!' The twine breaks where it was tied to the chicken's legs and whips back overhead as the cap trees spring back. In a few moments the waves disperse and calm settles back over the lily pads. Now silent, Elsie is still frozen in her position of terror.

Tommy grabs Elsie by the shoulders and lifts her up to a standing position. Looking into her face, he exclaims. "That is an alligator! Alligators are the kings of the marshes. No one messes with an alligator. No one of her right mind puts herself in a position where an alligator can mess with her!"

As Elsie regains her composure, Tommy continues. "House rule number four! Never forget house rules number one, two, and three!"

Tommy reaches down and takes Elsie by the hand.

"Come on. Let's get back to the house."

Once back at the house, Elsie goes straight to her room. She does not reappear until time for dinner. After the meal she stays in the kitchen to help Molly clean up. "Aunt Molly, are you afraid of that alligator?"

"It's a dangerous animal."

"Has anyone tried to kill it?"

"No. I have a 16-gauge shotgun. I don't think it would have much effect on that beast. Lawrence has a Colt-45. A well-placed shot from that gun might kill the alligator but one would have to get close enough to get off the right shot. The alligator doesn't let anyone get close enough to do that."

"Has the alligator ever come down here?"

"Not that we know of. Alligators roam about and hunt during the night. We have everyone inside after dark. Nevertheless Lawrence set up the house rules to make sure that we are all safe during the day."

Now more assured of her safety, Elsie returns to her room for a good night's sleep.

# CHAPTER 10

# THE KING

Over the next ten days, as Elsie becomes adjusted to life on an island with three other people, she notices that things she seldom took the time to look at take on more significance. A small patch of wildflowers blooms near the garden. Each day for the next four days she goes out to the garden at noon to observe as six white pedals unfold to reveal circular yellow centers, not smooth but granulated with brown 'prickles' protruding around the edges.

"Aw, dang! You won again!" protests Tommy at the end of another game of Scrabble. "Mom, is there such a word as s-c-h-e-l-r?"

"Maybe you should stay with dominoes," suggests a voice from another room. "Clean up in there. We are going swimming after lunch. It will give you a chance to cool down before your father comes home."

After all the game pieces have been returned to their proper boxes, Elsie retreats to her room. While lying on her bed, she entertains memories of her arrival to Lungraun's Island. She recalls the bridge, the building the conductor called a 'fortress' and the map on the wall at the train station in FC9. She picks up her diary, turns to a blank page, and constructs a map (see Figure 1 on next page).

About an hour after lunch Elsie and Tommy appear at the front door in their swimming clothes. Molly appears behind them but not dressed for swimming. She has an umbrella in one hand and her 16-gauge double-barreled shotgun in the other. She takes station on the bench at the end of the dock with the umbrella shading her from the mid-afternoon sun and the shotgun across her lap for a warning or for defense, depending on the need.

The children enter the water next to the dock and wade out to near its end, where the depth is about

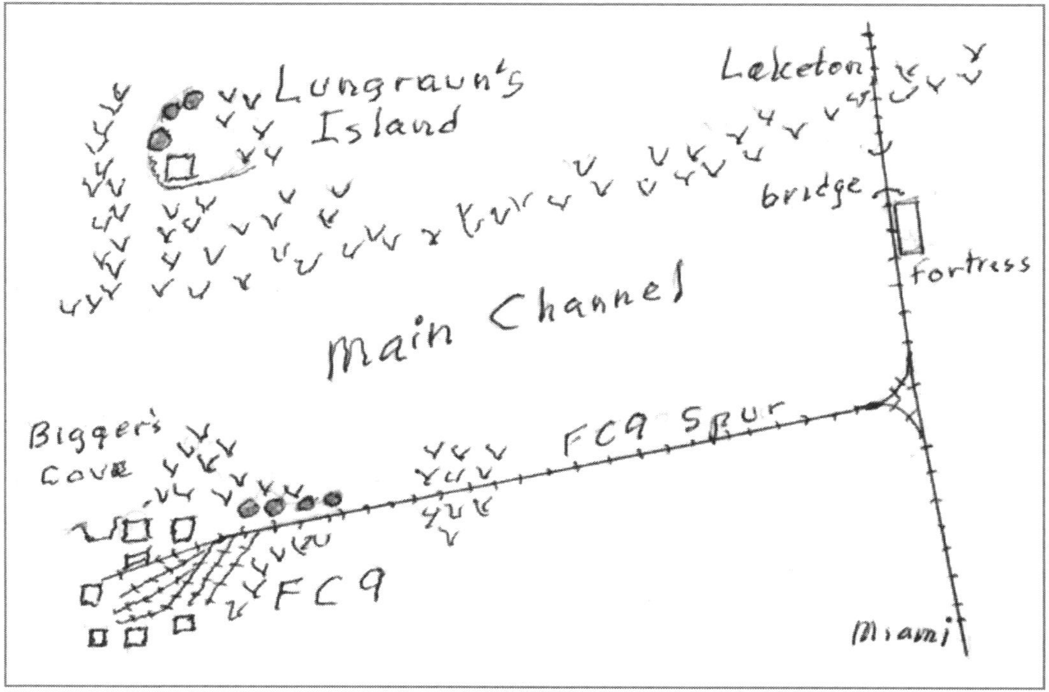
Lungraun's
Island
Leketon
bridge
Fortress
Main Channel
Bigger's
Cove
FC9 Spur
FC9
Miami

Figure 1

three feet. The water is about at body temperature and is so crystal clear as to be almost invisible, except that it creates a slight resistance as the children walk out farther.

With squeals of joy the children splash, swim, and throw water at each other. Meanwhile, Molly cowers under her umbrella to escape the direct sun. Finally she is relieved to be sitting in the coolness of shade as the sun goes behind a cloud. The water fight continues until Tommy recognizes he is being splashed by water that is not coming from Elsie's direction. He looks up at his mother and queries, "Why are you throwing water at me?"

Then he discovers that Molly is not throwing water at him. "It's beginning to rain!" he yells.

Both children struggle out of the water as quickly as they can and run for the house. Molly follows as large rain drops beat on her umbrella. Back at the house she laughs. "You've been in water, you've been throwing water on each other, and the moment rain falls on you, you run to the house as if you've been exposed to the plague."

Molly pauses for a moment then exclaims, "Oh!

Oh! Let's get to the pots and pans!"

All three race for the cabinets, grab what they can, and run to their rooms to place pots and pans over the white circles drawn on the floors. As the roof leaks, Elsie notices an almost musical sound. 'Plink, ding, plunk, dink, plink, plunk, ding, plink, plunk, ding, ding, plunk, dink, ding, plunk.'

When the rain finally stops, the three gather the pots and pans, drain and dry them, and return them to their special places to be ready for their next use. Later in the afternoon, they hear the distant sound of an outboard motor. "Hey, kids!" calls Molly. "Father is coming up the channel. He will need help unloading supplies. Hurry down to the dock to meet him."

Tommy and Elsie reach the bench at the end of the dock just in time to see the boat come into view down the channel. A minute later Lawrence steers his boat to a stop next to the dock. Tommy attaches the tie-down rope to a mooring post in front of the boat while Lawrence shuts down the motor and secures the rear of the boat to the dock. Then he hands up bags of supplies to two pair of waiting hands.

Meanwhile, Molly has begun preparations for

supper. As Lawrence and the kids finish bringing in supplies, Molly calls out, "Lawrence, please fetch some beans from the garden."

Lawrence heads for the back door from the kitchen. Still looking for something to do, Tommy follows. Elsie follows Tommy.

"SCREECH!"

Lawrence and Tommy freeze in their tracks.

"SCREECH!"

Startled by the high-pitched sound they turn around slowly, seeking from where it comes. Elsie is frozen in fear as she stares at the chicken coop.

"Elsie! What's wrong?" calls Tommy

"S-s-s-snake!" quakes Elsie as she points toward the base of the chicken coop.

Lawrence steps around Tommy and approaches the chicken coop as Elsie, still pointing, backs away. Along the ground just in front of the chicken coop lies the object of Elsie's terror. About five feet long and solid black with the exception of white rings spaced along its body, the snake lies motionless. Lawrence smiles and slowly squats down near the snake. It slithers forward about a foot and stops, its forked tongue testing the air. He lightly slides a knuckle along the snake's back. It turns, facing him, with its tongue darting in and out. Lawrence slowly slides his hand under the snake's midsection and lifts it from the ground. Then he drapes it over his arm to give it a more stable hold. As he turns around Elsie steps backward several feet.

"Elsie, meet Harry," says Lawrence softly. "Harry is a friend and a good reason we can live on this island. There were rattlesnakes and coral snakes here when we came. One of the workmen found Harry and gave him to us. Elsie, you and Harry share one thing in common. You both hate snakes."

Elsie straightens up a bit and her face relaxes.

Lawrence continues. "Harry is a King Snake. Once Harry moved in, the rattlesnakes disappeared."

Lawrence turns more toward Elsie so that the snake seems to look straight at her. She steps back further.

"Want to touch Harry?"

Elsie is having none of it.

"Okay. He lives under the chicken coop. You may see him from time to time, but he won't hurt you."

Lawrence slowly lowers the snake to the ground. It slithers away and disappears under the chicken coop.

## CHAPTER 11

# FOURTH OF JULY

At the evening meal on Sunday, the third of July, Lawrence makes an announcement. "Tomorrow is the Fourth of July. That means that almost everyone working on the railroad will be at FC9 for the celebrations. I think we should make a visible statement. We should go to town by mid-morning."

"Will we get to see any fireworks?" queries Elsie.

"No. We will have to leave FC9 by early evening to be back before it gets dark."

The next morning, after a robust breakfast, they gather on the dock. Lawrence boards first, then Molly hands him four empty water canteens to be returned to Sutton's store. Next she hands him her 16-gauge shotgun in its case, climbs aboard, and takes her place on the seat at the bow. Notably, she carries a box of shotgun shells in her bag.

Elsie boards while Tommy removes ropes from the mooring posts and gives the boat a shove as he boards. In short order the motor hums, Lawrence puts it in forward gear, and the dock and the cabin grow smaller.

It is the first time in over two weeks that Elsie has been off the island. She has grown familiar with grass and water, however the sight of side channels that disappear behind stands of grass still beckon to her curiosity as to just what may be hidden there.

Lawrence expertly guides their boat through the meandering channel toward FC9. After about fifteen minutes, the channel opens into the mile-wide main channel. Elsie can see what looks like the tops of man-made structures protruding above the stands of mangroves lining the shore. They disappear as their boat draws closer to Fletcher's Island. Then the arm of grass identifying Bigger's Cove reaches out to meet them.

Lawrence turns the boat to run parallel to Fletcher

Island until the opening to Sutter's harbor appears. He turns toward the entrance. Many boats are moored but there is space for Lawrence. As he ties down his boat, a man approaches. Shaggy brown hair leaks from beneath a cap that shields his eyes from the sun. His unkempt shirt and pants are dirt- and grease-stained. He stands on the dock waiting for Lawrence to finish tying down the boat and look up.

Lawrence disconnects the fuel line from the motor and sets the fuel tank on the dock. That's when he notices ankles protruding from a pair of shoes. Looking up, he smiles and then turns toward Elsie. "Elsie, this is the man who runs the place, Avery Sutton."

Sutton tips his hat toward Elsie and focuses on Lawrence, who continues. "Fill the tank and I want ten gallons of water in the canteens. Put it on my account."

Sutton grasps the handle of the fuel tank, picks up the straps of four canteens and proceeds down the dock. Tommy and Elsie scramble out of the boat followed by Molly, who gracefully disembarks then steps toward Lawrence, who hands her the shotgun case. Last of all, Lawrence climbs out of the boat and

Molly gratefully allows him to carry her shotgun.

'Bang!' 'Bang!' 'Bang' Elsie hears the noise of firecrackers before they leave the dock. The family steps up from the dock and walks toward the main street. There are tents and booths festooned with flags and hawkers selling just about anything, but mostly food and beer. About two-hundred people, all men ranging from just older than boys to ones with shades of grey on beards, some laughing and shouting, most consuming beer, are milling about contributing to the carnival atmosphere.

A voice calls Lawrence by name. He turns to Molly. "Take the children and get into line for lunch. I need to talk to the superintendent, Stan Faulkner. He turns and disappears while Molly herds Tommy and Elsie to a line that promises to lead to a tent where hotdogs are being cooked.

Many of the men have worked on the railroad long enough to have either met Molly or know who she is. They treat her with courtesy and give her space in the food line. Some of the newer employees who don't know her take their cue from the others.

Molly secures lunch for four and she and the

children rejoin Lawrence. They find an unoccupied bench in front of the hotel and enjoy their food while watching the atmosphere slowly change from celebration to mild intoxication.

Several times during the afternoon Molly finds herself alone when the children follow Lawrence. The mood changes from courtesy, to unwanted notice, to verbal suggestion. An individual with a beer in one hand who is having trouble walking proclaims, “Hey Sweetheart. What do you do all day on that island by yourself?”

Molly turns to face him. “Wanna find out?”

“Yeh,” the man returns with a sly smile.

“Then follow me over to the gun range.”

She waves to Lawrence who is standing with the children a short distance away. Then she proceeds toward the practice range followed by her obnoxious admirer and about a half-dozen others who, by this time, are bored with the usual activities. She arrives at the same time as does Lawrence, who is carrying her 16-gauge shotgun in its case. She lifts the gun out while the range operator, known only as ‘Mickey,’ sets up three targets at a range of fifty feet.

"Gather around, everybody," laughs one of the inebriated onlookers. "Annie Oakley is stepping up to the line."

'POW!' 'POW!' 'POW!' Mickey gathers up the targets and brings them back to Molly. "Nailed every one," he smiles.

Lawrence takes the targets and hands them to the crowd, which has grown to about fifteen. Then he calls out, "Mickey!"

Mickey turns around facing Lawrence, who raises four fingers on his right hand. Mickey can be heard commanding one of his workers. "Bradley, set up four birds for the lady!"

Molly walks a short distance to another part of the gun range. After standing for a few seconds, she yells, "Pull!"

'Thwaang!' A mechanical launcher hurls a clay disc outward and upward at high velocity. Molly lifts up her gun. 'POW!'

'Puff!' The clay disc turns to dust.

Three more times she yells, 'Pull!' Three more times the onlookers hear 'POW!' then see a small cloud of dust. Molly turns toward the crowd of onlookers and smiles.

"Only four tries," calls one of the onlookers. "Looks like you were only beginning to have fun."

"No fun here," smiles Molly. "This is only practice. The real fun begins when I get to take out some varmint crawling onto my island."

"C'mon, loudmouth!" Two companions take hold of the arms of the vocal drunk. "Let's get you out of here before she pins a target on your chest."

Molly turns toward Lawrence with a half-smile as she pulls the case over the shotgun.

Toward late afternoon the mood becomes more chaotic. Several fist fights have broken out. Someone has begun throwing firecrackers into the crowd and then laughing as others hop and jump to avoid explosions around their feet. It's time for the Lungrauns to head for home.

While exchanging pleasantries with acquaintances, they slowly make their way back to Avery Sutton's harbor. Sutton has resupplied the Lungrauns. They quietly board their boat and in a few minutes the motor hums as it pushes them out of the harbor.

Elsie looks back at FC9 as the tops of buildings reappear above the mangroves. With the sun sinking low in the west and the sounds of firecrackers diminishing, they leave the main channel and enter the side channel that takes them to their cabin.

After Molly assembles a robust dinner, Lawrence retreats to the bench at the end of the dock to enjoy his pipe in the fading twilight. He calls back to the cabin, "Hey, everybody. Come on out here. It looks like we are going to have fireworks after all."

The three walk out on the dock and notice Lawrence looking back over their heads behind them. Elsie's facial expression radiates awe as she steps next to Lawrence and turns to face east. A massive thunderstorm, rising in shades of grey, stands silhouetted against the dark of the oncoming night sky. The cloud is barely discernable when one looks low down toward the horizon. However its top still glows white in the fading twilight.

To Elsie the storm looks like a massive mountain. Hills in the foreground give way to foothills then to low mountains then eventually to the highest mountain with cliffs that cannot be climbed.

As darkness settles in, sections of the cloud light up as if frosted lamps are being turned on and off in rapid succession. Sometimes just a single lamp flashes. At other times a string of lamps flash, some horizontally through the cloud and others vertically, sometimes from the top of the storm all the way through its base and to the ground.

"How far away do you think the storm is?" queries Molly.

Lawrence replies, "At least twenty miles, probably more. I don't think we will hear much thunder."

Both Tommy and Elsie sit in awe as the light show goes on and on. Adding to the excitement is Elsie's observation that the light show is always a little different. The storm is constantly changing shape. Foothills become low mountains and low mountains become the body of the storm. Clouds in the foreground are silhouetted black against flashes of light in the background. That is, until those clouds become electrically charged.

But the greatest excitement is when lightning bolts break out of the cloud and streak down through open air, only to disappear behind clouds in the foreground then reappear below the bases of those clouds to strike the ground. Some bolts are smooth; some are jagged;

some break into forks. Some flash only once; others flash multiple times.

"Wow! Did you see that one!" exclaims Tommy.

Well, of course they did. They were all looking in the same direction.

After awhile Lawrence yawns. "Looks like this lightning show is going to go on for some time. But it's getting late and I have to be at work tomorrow. It's time we go to bed."

Elsie lies in her bed, staring at the far wall. Flashes of light coming through her window light up the room. As she imagines the distant storm, she wonders if this flash or that flash is the best display yet. Then she yawns and it is morning.

## CHAPTER 12

# FRESH DINNER

After breakfast on the morning of July eighteenth, Molly approaches Tommy. "I would like to have fresh fish for dinner tonight. Your father will be back. Would you and Elsie be so kind as to catch some brim this morning? I have some shelled corn and left-over pieces of meat you can use for bait."

Tommy finds Elsie in her room. "Elsie, want to go fishing?"

"No."

"Why not?"

"I don't fish. I think catching them is mean. And I really think cutting them up is awful."

Tommy stares at the floor for a moment while

trying to collect his thoughts. "Have you ever eaten fish?"

Elsie hesitates. "Yes."

Then she follows before Tommy can answer. "But they are already cut up and don't look like fish!"

"Does your mother buy them in a store or does your father catch fish?"

"Father has some friends who like to fish. He goes with them to catch fish. They do all the bad stuff before mother gets them."

"Hmmm. Suppose I take a bucket of water with us and we put all the fish we keep in the bucket. That means they will stay alive. So you won't see anything ugly. I will clean the fish by myself after we get back."

"Get back? Aren't you going to fish from the end of the dock?"

"No. There is a small pond in one of the side channels on the south side of the island."

"You don't have a boat. Your father has it at work. How will you get to this pond?"

"Come on. I'll show you."

Tommy leads Elsie out the front door toward the dock. Then he steps to the side toward a clump of grass. Mostly concealed in the grass is what looks like a large door. Tommy points to the wooden planks and proclaims. “When Dad built the cabin he had some wood left over so he made me this raft. Said we should have some means to navigate these waters if we needed to. Mom would never let me go out alone so the only times I went out were when she wanted to. We explored a nearby side channel that has lots of fish. If she wants me to go out and fish, she must be okay with it as long as you are with me.”

“Okay, I’ll go. But I won’t fish.”

“I have just the thing you can do. It gets real hot out there in the direct sun. I’ll take along an umbrella and you can use it to provide shade.”

They run back to the cabin. “You get an umbrella from Mom and I will get the fishing stuff.”

Tommy steps out by the chicken coop and locates a long wooden pole and his cane fishing pole. He finds a bucket under the back step. Smiling broadly while holding up the umbrella, Elsie meets Tommy as he drags his stuff through the kitchen. “Here, take the bucket!” commands Tommy as he hands it toward Elsie. As he drags his ‘poles’ through the kitchen, he picks up a small jar holding kernels of corn and small pieces of meat.

Elsie follows Tommy out the front door and closes it behind her. They set their gear down next to the raft. As he brushes sand from the top of the raft, Tommy laments, "Raft's been sitting here for a long time and has settled into the sand. It's gonna be tough to push it to the water. Could be snakes hiding underneath."

"Snakes!" screams Elsie as she backs away.

Tommy immediately regrets what he has just said. "Just kidding. No snakes. Too hot here. Anyway, watch where your feet are when we move it."

He slides the pole under one end of the raft to lift it as he pushes it toward the water. As no snakes slither from beneath it, Elsie gains courage to help with the pushing. By the time they get the raft to the edge of the water, they are gasping and perspiring. "Should be easier from here," encourages Tommy.

"I think I will be ready for a good swim when we get back," pants Elsie.

Tommy propels and steers by pushing the pole into the bottom sand from either the back or the sides of the raft. Elsie stays out of his way by sitting in front.

They move so slowly Elsie watches to see if she can see the grass grow. As they turn into the side channel, the only sense of going faster is that the channel is narrower and the grass along the edge is closer so that it is occasionally overrun by the raft.

Finally they come to a place where the channel widens into a circular pool. "The water gets a little deeper here," comments Tommy. "This is where we will fish."

They drift to the side where the grass holds them in place. Tommy fills the bucket with water, unfurls the line on the cane pole, and baits his hook. Elsie opens the umbrella to provide some much-needed shade. Tommy drops his line as far out as one can with a cane pole, sits down, and waits.

'Blip.' The bobber goes down. Tommy sets the hook and spends the next few minutes hanging on to his cane pole as a fish runs every which way below. Finally he wins and pulls up a bluegill larger than a grown man's hand. "Wow! This one's big!"

He carefully places the fish in the bucket, rebaits his hook, and returns to fishing. In short order he has landed two more bluegills of approximately the same size.

The next fish is smaller. Tommy removes the hook and tosses it back on the raft toward Elsie. "Pick it up and put it in the bucket."

'Flop, flop.' "Euw!" Elsie's ugly expression conveys exactly how she feels. 'Flop, flop.' Elsie slowly picks up the fish by its head. 'Wiggle, wiggle!' "Eeek!" She drops the fish. 'Flop, flop.' 'Splash!'

"You let it get away!" complains Tommy.

"Good enough!" retorts Elsie. "It deserved to get away."

In about a half hour, and despite Elsie, Tommy has six good-sized bluegills in his bucket. He poles the raft slowly back to the cabin. When they make landfall, Elsie is happy to step off the raft and hasten to the cabin.

Glad to be away from fish, Elsie returns to her room, relaxes on her bed, and opens her diary. Turning to a fresh page she writes her side of the fishing story. Then, summarizing her adventures since arriving on Lungraun's Island, she draws a map of the island and its environs. (see Figure 2 on next page)

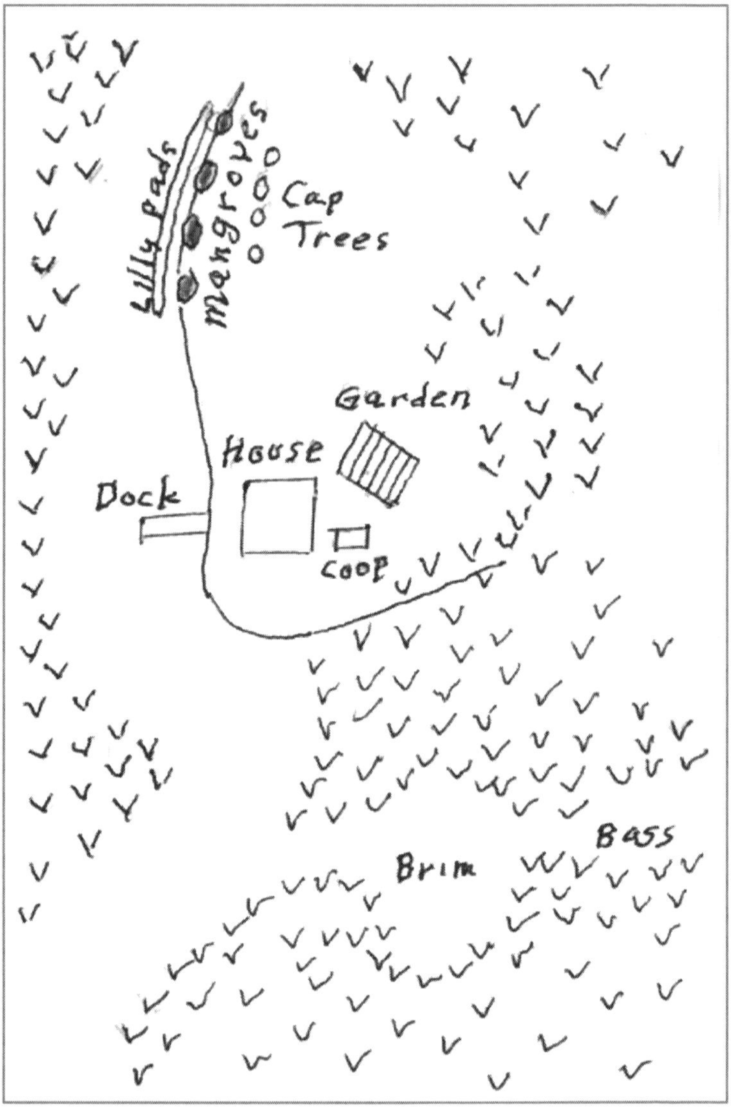
Lilly pads
Mangroves
Cap
Trees
Garden
House
Dock
coop
Brim
Bass

Figure 2

Later in the morning Tommy presents a delighted Molly with a gift consisting of a bowl of filleted fish. Then Tommy makes a request. Mom, Elsie and I worked real hard and got all sweaty getting the raft into the water. How about a swim this afternoon?

Smiling, Molly agrees.

# CHAPTER 13

# SKUNKED

After breakfast Elsie returns to her room to work on her diary. It is the first of August and her thoughts are being drawn to her departure for home in about ten days. On one hand, she will be happy to be back with her own family in the familiar surroundings of Canton. On the other hand, there is something about Lungraun's Island that has its own appeal.

She becomes lost in thought. *It's not that I went on some great adventure that would have my friends drooling with envy. Here I am in south Florida and I haven't gone to the beach one time. Perhaps it's just that life has slowed down. It's not that life has gone empty. Far from it! It's just that things we normally don't notice have become important. Six weeks of one summer on a small south Florida island. What could be different on each day? Well… clouds, wind, showers, and flowers.*

Elsie's thoughts are interrupted by Molly's voice. "Tommy. It looks like we are running low on foodstuffs. Father won't be back until evening day after tomorrow. I want you and Elsie to catch us some fish for lunch. We don't need as many as you caught the last time you were out since there are only the three of us."

"Okay, Mom. Will do. A good swim will be a nice reward. Yes?"

"Yes."

Before Tommy can call her name, Elsie stands in the kitchen doorway. He darts through the back door to grab the raft pole, the fishing pole, and the bucket. Elsie procures the umbrella. Tommy runs back through the kitchen, hands the bucket to Elsie, and secures the jar with corn and pieces of meat. Then they head for the raft.

This time the raft is easier to drag into the water. As Tommy 'poles' them slowly along the channel, Elsie takes note of her surroundings. Some of the morning coolness remains. The sky is deep blue and cloudless. There is no wind and the water is like glass. During her stay on Lungraun's Island she has become familiar with these mornings.

Tommy turns the raft up the side channel and they eventually find themselves at the deep pool. He guides the raft to the side, parks it in the grass just like before, and sets about baiting his hook. He places his line in the water and they wait with anticipation for the first taker. After awhile their anticipation slackens as nothing happens.

Tommy pulls in his line to check his bait. Nothing has bitten on it. He puts the line out in a different direction and waits. And keeps waiting. "Hmmm. Looks like things are a little slower than they were last time we where here."

The coolness of the late morning is gone. The sky is blue and cloudless and the water is as still as glass. Elsie unfurls the umbrella. Tommy pulls in his line again and changes the bait from corn to a piece of meat. He puts out his line in a different direction.

They wait. Tommy becomes fidgety. Still no bites; not a nibble. He pulls in his line. "Let's go to another part of the pond. Maybe something is biting over there."

With no wind, the heat is approaching limits of comfort. Tommy poles the raft slowly across the pond. The only disturbances on the water are the ripples produced by the raft. He stops over open water as there is no wind to push them into the grass. He rebaits his hook with corn, tosses his line into the water, and waits. After waiting for a time sufficient for fish to bite, he retrieves his line and throws it in a different direction from the raft.

Even with the shade from the umbrella, the heat is exceeding the limits of comfort. Finally Tommy gives up. "It's obvious that bluegills are not feeding today. There's a deep place in the channel where bass like to gather. Let's go there."

He poles the raft back across the pond and turns farther down the channel. After poling a few hundred feet he stops. He baits his hook with meat and puts his line as far forward from the raft as he can, up next to the grass. "Now let's see if we can tease a bass to come out of the grass."

After Tommy's three failed tries to lure a bass, Elsie raises an alarm. "Tommy. Given how hot it has become, it must be approaching noon. We are going to have to return soon if we are going to be back before lunch."

After several more tries to lure a bass out of the grass, Tommy gives up. "Yes. Let's go back."

Retracing their path back along the channel, through the pond, to the channel leading toward the cabin and the dock seems to take longer than it should have. The heat makes it so. Molly is waiting and welcomes them back. "Given the time, I figured you were not having much in the way of luck out there so I went ahead and prepared pancake mix. Come in and have some lunch."

Tommy smiles at the prospect of pancakes.

While they wait for the first pancakes, Elsie retreats to her room and opens her diary to the page where she had drawn her map of Lungraun's Island (Figure 2). Taking her pen she adds an extension to the side channel where they had caught the bluegills and labels it 'bass.'

After lunch and toward mid-afternoon, as the

cabin temperature becomes unbearable, Molly looks out toward the dock. The dock seems to rest on a plate of perfectly blue glass. "Strange," she whispers to herself loud enough for Tommy and Elsie, who are sitting nearby, to hear. "Strange there has been no wind for the whole day."

"And no clouds," follows Elsie.

Now in a louder and more motherly voice Molly replies. "Let's go out for a swim."

As has become routine when the cabin gets hot, Elsie and Tommy don their swim clothes and follow Molly, who carries her umbrella and shotgun. The temperature of the water is not much cooler than the temperature of the air. The children frolic in the water at the end of the dock while Molly surveys the channel for ripples identifying an approaching snake, or, worse, the slow movement of a 'log' that happens to have a long tail and lots of teeth.

As the late afternoon shadows cast by stands of grass on the opposite side of the channel begin to spread toward them, Molly calls a halt to the swim party. She needs time to make biscuits and to figure out what to add to make an evening meal. As the children step out of the water ahead of her she calls to Tommy. "Tommy. After you have changed clothes, please go out into the garden and pick some beets. We will have beets and beet leaves for salad tonight."

After dinner, Tommy and Elsie retreat to the bench at the end of the dock. Molly is doing the usual post-meal cleanup. Suddenly she stops as thoughts overflow her mind. *I don't like this day! We are running low on supplies. Tommy went fishing and got skunked! Tommy always comes home with plenty of fish. Why not today? Why did this happen when we are low on supplies? And this weather! No wind for the entire day. And no clouds! Since we have been on this island this has never happened. Something seems not quite right. I don't like this day!*

Even though there is nothing to do after the lanterns are turned off, Elsie doesn't feel like going to bed. The night is still. There is no call from a distant owl. Not even a chirp from an insect. Her room is unbearably hot. The mosquito net curtain over her window hangs limp. The only air movement is from her breathing. Elsie stirs to find the least uncomfortable position and eventually falls into a shallow sleep.

## CHAPTER 14

# MISSING GATOR

After breakfast Molly addresses the children. "Since you didn't catch fish yesterday, it's going to be hard to put together lunch for today. Why don't you try again? Perhaps fish will be biting today."

Somewhat disinterestedly Tommy replies. "Okay. We'll go."

Clearly not in a hurry, Tommy gathers his equipment as before. Just as he and Elsie are about to leave the cabin for the raft, Tommy calls to Molly. "Mom, I have an idea. Do you know where Dad keeps his aquaviewer?"

"It's back in his room. I will get it for you."

Shortly, Molly appears with a cone-shaped bucket with a glass bottom. Then Tommy and Elsie are on their way to the raft.

As Tommy 'poles' them slowly along the channel, Elsie once again takes note of her surroundings. The sky is deep blue and cloudless. There is no wind and the water is like glass. She is not looking forward to another day like yesterday.

Tommy poles them up the side channel and they eventually glide into the deep pool. He guides the raft to the side and parks it in the grass just as before. Then he sets about baiting his hook. He tosses his line in the water and for a while the two watch the bobber. Nothing happens.

Tommy sets his cane pole on the raft and reaches for the aquaviewer. While lying on his stomach, he presses the glass end into the water. As the water is clear, his line and hook look like they are suspended in air. He turns from one side of the raft to the other. He looks toward deep water then toward the shallow water near the grass. Then he exclaims. "No wonder we didn't catch anything yesterday; there's nothing here! Not even a minnow! I can see the grass in the sand at the bottom. There is nothing here!"

He sets the aquaviewer on the raft, sits up and looks at Elsie. "Let's see if there are fish on the other side."

Leaving his line in the water, he poles the raft to the other side of the pond. Then, lying on his stomach, he pulls the aquaviewer in front of him and surveys the bottom. "There's nothing here, Elsie! Not a fish; not a crab; not a worm. Nothing!"

Tommy sits up and pulls in his line. "Let's go back down the channel to where the bass are. Usually there are small fish there. That's why the bass like to be there."

He poles the raft back across the pond and turns further down the channel. After poling a few hundred feet he stops. On his stomach again and with the aquaviewer at his face, Tommy surveys the bottom of the channel. "Nope! Nothing! Not even a small minnow."

They retrace their route back along the channel through the pond to the channel leading toward the cabin. Now, in a wider expanse of water, Elsie observes her surroundings. The sky overhead is cloudless and deep blue. The grass hangs limp and the water is like a mirror. As they approach the dock Tommy's face seems to harden. They beach the raft and enter the cabin, putting away things they have taken. "No fish today, Mom!" he exclaims.

"Why not?" queries Molly firmly.

"The place is empty. There are no fish there. There is nothing to catch."

"That seems strange," she replies.

Still with a hardened expression, Tommy exits the back door, produces his pocketknife and proceeds toward the spool of twine. He cuts an approximate fifteen inch length of twine and steps toward the chicken coop. Pointing to a certain chicken he mumbles. "This one ought to do."

"What are you doing?" queries Elsie, now alarmed by past memories.

Tommy doesn't answer. He pulls a chicken out of the coop and ties its legs with the twine. Elsie cajoles, "Just because you are angry about no fish, you can't take it out on that poor chicken!"

Holding the chicken under his left arm Tommy

glares at Elsie. "Follow me!"

He takes a pole and prods his way through the stands of grass toward the distant cluster of mangrove trees. Elsie protests. "Look, I already know house rule number four!"

They reach the mangroves and the patch of lily pads that sit as silent and motionless sentinels on the placid channel just offshore. Tommy prods the sand with the pole as he walks back and forth among the trees. Finally the pole pulls up a loose length of twine. Tommy studies the twine. "Hmmm. This looks like its still good enough to use."

He pulls the twine until he comes to the loose end. Then he puts the chicken on the ground and ties the twine to its already bound legs. Carrying the chicken, he follows the line to where it links with the line tied between the two 'cap trees.' That twine looks to be in good shape also. He calls out, "Elsie, come over here and take the chicken back to where you were when we launched the last one."

"NO! I will not be part of your killing another chicken!"

"Okay! Then I'll do it myself!"

Tommy steps farther into the grass, pulling the tops of the trees toward him. Then he puts the chicken on the ground and steps back to where he can continue pulling the trees down. Elsie rushes past him, picks up the chicken and grasps it tightly against her chest. "No! I will not let you kill this chicken!"

Tommy holds the trees down. "Let go!" he commands.

"No!"

Tommy looks back at her and scowls. Elsie stands resolutely with the chicken pressed against her chest. Then she is perplexed as Tommy's expression suddenly changes. "What is that black thing on your hair behind your left ear? It's a bug! A big bug!"

"Eeek! Where?" Elsie moves the chicken to under her left arm to free up her right arm to swat at the bug. "Where is it?"

"You missed it. It's further back!"

She swats her hair again while loosening her hold on the chicken. Tommy releases the trees.

'Swoosh!'

"Twang!"

'Squawk!' 'Squawk, squawk, squawk!'

"Hey!"

Elsie looks up to see the chicken flying away. "You rat!" she screams as she runs toward Tommy. He looks up with satisfaction to see the chicken catapulted about 50 feet overhead toward the water. She arrives at his side just in time to hunch over in terror, her mouth agape, grasping her jaw with her hands as the bird, squawking and flapping its wings to brake its fall, settles in the water just beyond the lily pads.

'Splosh!' 'Splosh!' The chicken attempts to flap its wings to stay afloat. Then it struggles forward a few inches to grasp a lily pad with its beak.

Elsie's posture of terror slowly dissolves as she releases her jaw and stands erect. Tommy's expression changes to wide-eyed bewilderment. He slowly steps forward, taking hold of the line of twine to the chicken from where it drops down from the line connecting the two trees. He stops as Elsie screams. "Don't you go near that water! That monster may be there waiting to grab you!"

Tommy slowly pulls the line toward himself as he watches the chicken struggle and splash water from the edge of the lily pads all the way to the shore. He drags the chicken from the shore, past the mangrove trees, then onto the grass-spotted sandbar on which he stands. He picks up the wet chicken and with his pocket knife severs the connecting line. Then, without a word, he and Elsie walk slowly back to the cabin.

They return in time to put the chicken back in its coop and go to eat the lunch fragments Molly has been able to assemble. They go swimming during the afternoon and the waves they make from kicking and splashing are the only disturbances on the placid waters.

Late that evening, well after the sun has set, Elsie wanders down to the dock. Standing next to the bench she surveys her surroundings. With little to no light to reflect, the water looks like undisturbed black glass. A cloud runs just above the southeastern horizon. Pale white against the night sky, the cloud must be very high to be reflecting what's left of twilight. Elsie turns toward the cabin.

Tonight is just like last night. Her room is unbearably hot. The only air movement is from her breathing. Elsie finally finds a comfortable position and eventually falls into a shallow sleep. Sometime during the night, most likely after midnight, the mosquito net curtain over her window moves slightly. Then it stops. Sometime later it moves again, this time with persistence. Sensing the coolness that has invaded her room, Elsie falls into a deep sleep.

CHAPTER 15

# LAWRENCE RETURNS

After breakfast Molly comes to Elsie with a request. "With no fish for the past two days, I am really pressed to come up with something for lunch. Thank God Lawrence will be home with supplies for dinner. But for lunch would you be willing to go out to the garden to see if there is anything we could eat. Ripe tomatoes, beans, carrots, squash. Anything?"

"Yes, ma'am."

Elsie departs through the back door and walks carefully past the chicken coop toward the garden. She does not want to be surprised by any snakes. Searching through the garden she picks up three small ripe tomatoes and one squash.

She also notices that the white cloud she saw late last evening has risen higher in the southern and eastern sky. It almost covers the early morning sun, but Elsie can see the sun's disc shining through the thin wisps. Most of the grass stands motionless, but a few blades meander slowly in a breeze almost too light to be felt.

Elsie places her loot on the kitchen table and seeks out Tommy. He has no appetite for fishing or swimming so they spend their time playing dominoes and scrabble until Molly calls them for lunch.

The two resume their games after lunch. By mid-afternoon Tommy has tired of losing at scrabble so Elsie retreats to her room. As she lies on her bed reviewing entries in her Diary, a faint yet familiar sound works its way into her mind. The sound is coming from outside. She crawls down from her bed and pushes aside the mosquito net curtain from the window. The sound is from wind blowing through the grass.

Several hours later Elsie hears a different sound, the hum of an outboard motor. She climbs down from her bed and joins Tommy and Molly as they head toward the end of the dock. Lawrence has returned.

Lawrence hands the tie-downs to Tommy, who quickly secures the boat to the dock. "Quick, children!" commands Molly. "Carry the food stuffs back to the cabin."

Tommy and Elsie grab several burlap bags and tote them off the dock. With her dress flapping between her legs and some of her hair blowing across her face Molly exclaims to Lawrence. "My, my! It's gotten breezy. Did you have any trouble coming home?"

Lawrence smiles. "It was a little rough crossing the main channel but, overall, no, it wasn't bad."

The boat is unloaded and all return to the cabin to prepare for the evening meal. Molly unpacks the foodstuffs to get an overview of what she has to work with. Then she commences to prepare the meal.

As has been a longstanding after-dinner tradition, Lawrence retreats to the bench at the end of the dock for a smoke from his pipe. He cups his hands to shield a lit match as he draws the flame into the bowl. In a few moments a puff of blue smoke drifts swiftly over the channel and dissipates. Now he can soothe his thoughts and survey his surroundings.

Something is not quite right. Three summers on a small island at the perimeter of the south Florida Everglades teaches one a lot about the weather. The pattern is simple: Clear, calm, and relatively comfortable mornings grade into puffy clouds, light breezes, and hot afternoons. On some days the clouds produce showers and, on other days, they don't. Then the sun goes down, the clouds go away, and the wind stops.

That's not what had happened the past three days. It is past sundown, headed toward nightfall. The wind should be slacking. Instead, if anything, it seems the wind has gotten stronger.

And the cloud! True, the sun set clear. But that cloud is coming up from the southeast. Lawrence looks toward the southwest, turns to overhead, and then toward the northeast. The cloud covers more than half of the sky. Now bathed in shades of white, yellow, and orange, the entire southeastern half of the sky seems to glow. The size of the cloud is awesome!

Lawrence follows the cloud from overhead down to the southeastern horizon. Just above the horizon, barely visible in the fading twilight, is a long line of towering clouds, much like the clouds that produce showers during the afternoon. *But, why now? Why are those clouds building now?*

His thoughts are interrupted by the sound of Tommy walking onto the dock. Lawrence draws from his pipe and studies Tommy as he approaches. Tommy stands at his side and for a few moments there is silence. Then Lawrence speaks. "Your mother told me you got skunked yesterday."

"Can't catch fish if there ain't no fish."

Lawrence's focus narrows on Tommy. "What do you mean by 'no fish'?"

"Actually I got skunked the day before yesterday. I went out again yesterday, but this time I brought along your aquaviewer. Went back to the same places we fished before and viewed the water. No fish! Not even a minnow."

Lawrence looks up above Tommy's head almost as if he is ignoring him. Then Tommy continues more forcefully. "Dad! The gator's gone!"

Lawrence stiffens and stands motionless like a statue. Not sure he has been heard, Tommy repeats himself. "The gator's gone! I took a chicken up to the mangroves and threw it out beyond the lily pads. Nothing happened. The gator is not there."

Still staring over Tommy, Lawrence raises his right hand slowly to his face and lowers the pipe from his mouth. He speaks at almost a whisper. "This morning someone brought word that the Miccosukee Indians had left their village and moved deeper into the Everglades."

"Huh?"

Molly's voice is heard above the rustling of the wind in the grass. "Tommy! It's time for bed."

Leaving Lawrence in his statue-like stance, Tommy turns and runs off the dock toward the cabin.

Lawrence lifts the pipe back to his mouth, inhales, then exhales a small cloud of blue smoke. He removes the pipe and whispers again. "They had to have a reason for leaving."

He speaks louder as he walks off the dock. "A very good reason!"

Now ready for bed, Elsie notices the mosquito net window curtain swirling into her bedroom. She closes her window half way and climbs into bed. Then she falls asleep.

Sometime during the night Elsie is startled awake by the sudden roar of heavy rain falling on the roof of the cabin. There are several flashes of lightning followed by rumbles of thunder. The tempest passes and the out-of-doors becomes quiet. Then Elsie hears a faint voice from their bedroom as Lawrence speaks to Molly. "Maybe that's the end of it."

CHAPTER 16

# DEPARTURE FOR FC9

Tommy stands at her door. "Elsie! Get up and get dressed quickly. We are having an early breakfast. Dad is taking us to town."

Elsie almost jumps out of bed. As she gets dressed she notices sounds she has not heard before. Sounds of rafters creaking over head. It is raining lightly. No one seems to notice or care that, here and there, little droplets of water from the ceiling splash on the floor.

Elsie devours her breakfast in an atmosphere of urgency. Lawrence finishes first and Molly sweeps his placeware off the table and into the sink. He leaves the table in search of rain gear for four. Empty water canteens are already stacked by the door. There is no conversation.

Molly hovers over the table as the two children gobble. Each plate or glass or spoon that is no longer needed is swept away.

As soon as the children have finished Lawrence plops raingear on the table. "Okay, there's one for everyone. Let's put them on and get going. The sooner the better."

Tommy and Elsie find their raincoats and put them on. Molly is distracted. Lawrence barks a command. "No need to wash the dishes, Molly. We can do that when we get back."

Tommy and Elsie exit the cabin first. As she steps away, Elsie finds the wind pushing her toward the dock faster than she desires. Raindrops splatter against her back making so much sound that she can hear nothing else. She slows down and climbs aboard the boat as safely as she can, sitting facing toward the back to shield her face from the wind.

Lawrence gathers the water canteens and heads out the door. "Wait!" exclaims Molly. "I forgot something."

She rushes back inside to the bedroom closet, extracts a small cardboard box, and removes the lid.

Then she lifts from the box her most prized possession, her mother's pearl necklace, and places it in her purse.

As Molly leaves the cabin, Lawrence, already in the boat, starts the motor. Tommy waits at the edge of the dock to help Molly into the boat. With rain splattering her back, she quickly climbs aboard, taking her seat at the bow.

Tommy tries to release the tie-downs, but the wind, pushing the boat backward, holds the lines taut. Lawrence quickly discerns Tommy's dilemma and shifts the motor to 'forward' to counter the wind. As the boat moves forward the tie-down lines go slack, and Tommy unhooks them and quickly climbs aboard while the wind pushes the boat backward and away from the dock.

The bank of tall grass bordering the channel violently whips back and forth. A consolation is that the grass acts as a brake that lessens the force of the wind blowing across the channel. Elsie turns in her seat so she can face forward. As they pass the side channel to the fishing pond, she can feel the wind push the boat to the side. Lawrence quickly regains control.

The rain stops. Breaks in fast-moving low clouds reveal higher clouds above. As they reach the main channel, Elsie sees a grey waterscape of white-capping waves. Lawrence abruptly changes course, hitting full speed and turning the boat directly into the wind to take the waves head-on. The waves lift the bow and then slam the boat into the next wave. Molly is taken by surprise. She is almost knocked off her seat. Quickly she grabs the sides to steady herself.

For several minutes they endure the pounding until Lawrence abruptly turns the boat into the trench between two lines of waves. The move is a stroke of genius. The pounding stops and the wave rising up on the left blocks the wind. Lawrence skillfully maneuvers the boat down the trench; the only sounds now are the hum of the motor and the occasional slosh of a breaking white cap on their left.

It begins to rain again and Elsie turns her head to shield her face. She notices that the waves are becoming smaller, but that exposes her more to the wind-driven rain. The rain slackens and she hears a distant roar. She turns to see heaving branches of mangrove trees dead ahead. They have made it to Bigger's Cove.

Lawrence turns the boat to run parallel to the mangroves thus putting the rain and the wind to the backs of the passengers. After a few minutes a channel appears on their left. Lawrence executes another sharp turn and they enter the relatively placid, wind-sheltered waters of the harbor.

Save for their boat, the harbor is empty. Lawrence steers toward that part of the dock next to the looming side of Sutten's Dock & Marine Supply. He holds the boat steady while Tommy secures the mooring lines then shuts down the motor.

In the relative silence Elsie takes a deep breath and relaxes. They have arrived at Fletcher Camp Nine.

## CHAPTER 17

# UNPLEASANT DISCOVERY

Given the wind and rain, Lawrence doesn't expect to see Sutton coming to his boat. He hands the empty canteens to Tommy, disconnects the hose to the fuel tank, and lifts the tank onto the dock. Then he climbs out of the boat to join the others. Carrying his fuel tank, he leads the way to the door of Sutton's store. They enter into an office area where there are some chairs and a counter.

Molly and the children slump into the chairs. Lawrence stands at the counter. Avery Sutton does not appear, nor does his helper. "Avery!" Lawrence calls out. "Sutton, are you here?"

His call is not answered. "Hmmm," he ponders.

"Maybe Sutton is out in the shop near the back and he can't hear me because of the wind."

He steps around the counter and proceeds into a stockroom filled with marine supplies of all kinds. Then he walks out into the main shop area. 'Wheeooowheeooo' comes a sound from rafters high above him. "Sutton! Are you here?"

There is no reply.

Lawrence enters a bulk-storage room in the back. It is dark and void of human presence. Leaving there he shouts, "Avery!"

He finds a set of stairs to an upstairs office. The desk, books, and ledgers all seem to be in order. Except for one. The ledger for this year is missing.

Lawrence leaves the office and returns to the front counter where his family is waiting for him. "Well, it's clear that Sutton is nowhere to be found."

"What are we going to do?" queries Molly.

"Perhaps I can fill the water and fuel myself."

'Creak!' 'Groan!' 'Wheeooo!'

Molly studies Lawrence's face. "Honey, is something wrong?"

"Not sure, but something is not right."

Lawrence's eyes narrow in thought. "I have an idea."

He turns toward Tommy. "Tommy. You and Elsie run over to the hotel and see if anyone is there."

"Okay. Come on, Elsie."

The two cross the street toward the hotel in the roar of the wind through nearby mangrove trees. A few gusts buffet them, but for the most part they are protected from the full force of the gale. They enter the hotel and find no one. As they stand before the reservation desk, Tommy has an idea. He climbs behind the counter and retrieves keys to Rooms 211 and 212. "Come on. Let's go upstairs."

Elsie chases Tommy up the stairs to the second floor. They walk down the hallway to the sounds of creaking and groaning. The two rooms are located at the far end of the hall. Tommy keys the door and they enter Room 211. This room faces east and south. The carpet is soaked and a small puddle of water covers part of the floor. Water stains the window sill and parts of the wall below the east window.

Tommy steps around the water and pushes away the curtain covering the south window. His eyes widen as he looks out over the switchyard. "Holy cow! There's nothing there!"

He turns toward Elsie. "Come on. Let's look out of Room 212!"

They leave the room and open the door across the hall. This room views to the south and west. With eyes wide, Tommy exclaims. "The switchyard is empty! Let's get back to Mom and Dad!"

Tommy jumps down the stairs three or four steps at a time. Followed by Elsie, he bangs through the front door and out onto the street, to be buffeted again by wind and rain. They both cover their faces as best they can as they race toward Sutton's store. Panting as he enters Sutton's office three steps ahead of Elsie, Tommy exclaims, "Dad! They are all gone! Everything is gone!"

"Okay, okay," counsels Lawrence calmly. "Settle down and tell me what you mean."

Tommy gasps for breath and tries again. "We got to the hotel and there was nobody there. So I got some keys and went upstairs to rooms that look out over the switchyard."

Tommy almost yells, "Dad! The trains are all gone!

All the engines and all of the cars! They even took the old switch engine!"

Lawrence stares at Tommy for a moment. Then he proclaims, "They've evacuated!"

"What do you mean?" queries Molly, now alarmed.

"There were eighty men in FC9 last night. Someone must have come in and ordered them out. The fact that they took the old switch engine with them is revealing."

"Revealing of what?"

"Let's just say that they were considering the possibility that they might not be coming back."

"Well, we can stay here, can't we? We will be safe here, won't we?"

"Maybe. Then maybe not."

Lawrence looks at Molly firmly. "Molly. It's true that the winds are stronger than anything we have experienced since moving to Florida. It's also true that we successfully made our way across the main channel to FC9. We really don't know what's out there! But somebody knows more than we do. That somebody sent word to get everyone off FC9."

Lawrence pauses as Molly's eyes search him for

any signs of encouragement. Then he continues. "If FC9 is not safe for eighty men, FC9 is not safe for us."

"Then, where will we go?"

Lawrence lowers his eyes and speaks more softly. "There is one place we could go."

"The fortress?"

"Yes. The fortress. But getting there will be tough. We have to go seven miles up the main channel against the wind. That won't be easy."

Lawrence watches as the fear in Molly's eyes slowly evaporates into resolve. "I have a plan. I will get fuel and water here. Molly, you take the children over to the general store and stock up on food. You've done this before. Plan for three days of camping. We need energy food. Lightweight stuff we can carry in the boat. Chocolates, candy, peanut butter bars, dried meat, anything that's wrapped to withstand water. No jars or cans. Bring it all over here. Sutton has burlap bags and some waterproof bags."

Molly stares at Lawrence for a moment then turns. "Children, let's run!"

"Be fast!" exclaims Lawrence. "We are almost out of time!"

As Molly and the two children disappear out the door, Lawrence turns to his part of the preparation. After carrying his fuel tank back into the shop area, he locates Sutton's fuel station and fills the tank. Then he sees two other empty fuel tanks and fills these also. After cutting a strand of rope from a large spool, he carries the three fuel tanks to the boat and ties them to the bottom. He attaches the fuel hose from his tank to the motor, primes the line, and starts the motor. The motor hums beautifully.

Lawrence shuts down the motor and returns to Sutton's shop area, gathering up the four water canteens as he walks through the office. He locates Sutton's fresh water tank and refills the canteens. Then he takes the canteens back to the boat and secures them to the bottom.

Now back in the office, Lawrence slumps in a chair as he ponders his greatest challenge. It is a seven mile trip up the main channel to the fortress. He will have to face waves much of the way, waves larger than any he has ever encountered. But the greatest challenge will be the wind. A wind this strong will turn the boat if it hits the boat at an angle. Once the boat is turned, he will not have the power to turn the boat back against the wind. He will be captured – forced to go only downwind away from the fortress and into disaster.

So he must keep the boat headed into the wind at all times. But that presents a problem. The wind is blowing from the east, directly down the main channel. The means he must drive the boat to the east. However, FC9 is on the south side of the channel. The fortress and its bridge are on the north side of the channel. If he can drive the boat to the railroad embankment on the south side of the channel, how can he steer the boat a half mile to the north across the channel to the railroad embankment at the fortress? An idea comes to mind.

He gets up and walks back into the stockroom. He wanders down each aisle studying the objects on the shelves. Finally he finds what he is looking for – a three-pronged anchor. He pulls the anchor off the shelf and looks it over. *Yes, it is just the right weight and right size. It should do.*

He carries the anchor back into the shop area and measures out one hundred feet of rope. He attaches one end of the rope to the anchor then coils up the rope and carries the anchor back through the store toward his boat. As he passes through the stockroom his eyes fall on another treasure – a pair of safety glasses.

With the safety glasses shielding his eyes from the driving rain, Lawrence ties the free end of the rope to the front of the boat, carefully lays the remaining rope over the seats along one side, and places the anchor on the bottom within reaching distance of his seat at the back.

Lawrence manages a small smile. All is ready.

Molly and the children return with a large cart full of groceries. Fruits that don't mind water and waterproof packages go into the burlap bags. The remainder goes into the waterproof bags and then the bags are tied shut. Molly and Elsie remain in the office while Lawrence and Tommy carry the bags out to the boat and tie them in securely. Then they return to Sutton's office.

"Okay," begins Lawrence. "I think everything is tied down securely enough that the wind will not be able to blow them out. This is going to be a rough ride. Molly, find a comfortable place to sit on the bottom just below your seat. You will be sheltered from the wind there. Same for you, Elsie. Get down with the bags of groceries where you can be comfortable and sheltered. Not you, Tommy. I want you on your seat facing me. I will need your help. Your back will be to the wind. Anchor your feet among bags that are tied down so the wind will not be able to blow you out of the boat."

Lawrence stands and smiles. "Let's go."

Resolutely they file out of Sutton's office onto the dock. They are sheltered from the gusts but they can hear the roaring of the wind blowing through nearby mangroves. It is louder than it was when they arrived.

Molly and Elsie find their places on the bottom of the boat. Tommy releases the tie-downs. Lawrence puts on his safety glasses. The motor hums and the boat turns away from the dock. As they proceed to the far end of the harbor, gusts of wind push them on. Then Lawrence turns the boat toward the outlet.

## CHAPTER 18

# RIDE TO THE FORTRESS

As soon as they clear the entrance to the harbor Lawrence opens full throttle and gets the boat turning before the wind slams into its side. The waves are white-capping but they are not large since the fetch is from Bigger's cove. Lawrence brings the boat to full speed in these waves and executes a strategy to hit the larger waves just right to turn the boat slightly toward the main channel. Once there he corrects to head into the wind before the gale can generate enough force to turn the boat. He must move about a half mile into the channel before he can clear the arm of the cove.

Each movement toward the channel exposes

them to larger waves. Crouching on the bottom of the boat near the bow, Molly feels the full force of the waves. At first she can hear periodic 'sloshing' as the boat plows through the rough water. Then she begins to feel a 'thump' and a slight drop in speed. The 'thumps' get harder. Suddenly, she feels airborne and then 'slam!' She is pressed to the bottom of the boat as the bow plunges into a trough between towering waves. Hardly has she regained her bearings when she feels pressed again as the boat rises into the next wave.

Lawrence sees that he has cleared the arm of Bigger's cove and is now in the open main channel. His one task is to keep the boat headed straight into the wind, regardless of waves. The bow cuts through the top of the next ridge and descends toward the trough, pulling the stern out of the water and exposing the propellers. 'Fraaappp!'

It is starting to rain. A mixture of rain and spray from wind-blown whitecaps whips across the boat. Tommy wraps his legs in the burlap bags strapped to the bottom of the boat and braces himself against the wind, which is trying to blow him off his seat as the boat violently drops behind him and then rises equally violently.

Now the wind has substance. Wind-driven rain slams his back. Tommy looks at Lawrence sitting on the stern seat facing into the rain with his safety glasses. He looks more like a statue than a man. He seems frozen is his position and his facial expression is grim. Rain splashes over his safety glasses and runs down his cheeks giving him a shiny appearance.

'Fraaapp!' 'Wham! 'Fraaapp!' 'Wham! 'Fraaapp!' 'Wham!

The boat seems to be cutting through the waves instead of going over them. A wave begins to break as the boat cuts through and water pours into the boat. For the first time since they left FC9 Lawrence changes his expression, turns, and yells at Tommy over the howling of the wind. "Tommy! There is a can by my feet! It's time to start bailing!"

Tommy sees the can, falls to his knees, grabs it, and scoops water from the bottom of the boat as fast as he can. Just as it seems that he is making progress, another wave breaks over the sides of the boat adding more water to be bailed out. He bails until the muscles in his arms give out. Then he drops the can and slumps on his seat.

'Bam!' The bow of the boat drops into a trough just as the next wave breaks. A wall of water splashes across the boat and they are swamped. Tommy looks up. The stern is under water. All he can see is the top of the motor and Lawrence, sitting waist deep in water, his safety glasses covering his eyes, posture and expression unchanged, as if he is unaware of what has just happened. He can feel the boat slowing down.

Then the bow rises at the approach of the next wave. This wave seems to push the boat with it as the boat climbs toward the crest. Suddenly, the water in the boat surges past Tommy and flows out over the stern around Lawrence. The boat was swamped and now it isn't. But for how long?

The wave doesn't break. Tommy feels the bow dropping behind him. 'Fraaapp!' Then he feels a surge in forward speed as the propellers engage the crest of the departing wave. He falls on his knees, seizes the can, and with all the energy he can summon, he bails furiously, throwing the remaining water over the stern, much of it in the face of his father.

'Fraaapp!' 'Wham! 'Fraaapp!' 'Wham! 'Fraaapp!'

‘Wham!

The rain stops. The waves are still large but nothing like they were a half hour ago. Lawrence leans forward and taps Tommy on the knee. As Tommy looks up at his father, Lawrence smiles. “Tommy, we are approaching the railroad embankment. To keep the wind from turning us I’m going to ram the boat into the embankment.”

Tommy turns around to see winds whipping strips of foam from relatively small whitecaps. Then he turns to his father, who hands him the triple-hook boat anchor. “Carry this anchor up to the tracks and put one of the hooks over the rail at a plate that joins two rails. I will pull the boat back and let the wind take over. Then using tension from this rope I can turn the boat to run parallel to the embankment then ram it back into shore farther up. Once I’ve secured the boat, remove the anchor and set it up just as before, but farther down the tracks at another joint. Do you understand what I’m telling you?”

“Yes.”

“It’s critical that the anchor doesn’t get loose from the rail.”

"I understand."

"Run low or the wind will throw you back into the water."

'Bump!' "Oh!" exclaims Molly in surprise at the jolt.

Tommy rolls over the side into the shallow water next to the boat. He half crawls as he staggers ashore and fights his way toward the tracks while keeping a low profile so that the wind can't turn his raincoat into a sail. He struggles up the embankment and places the anchor with one of its hooks over the rail next to a connection plate. Then he waves at his father.

Lawrence cuts the motor to idle. As the wind pushes the boat back away from the embankment and turns it toward downwind, the hundred-foot length of rope plays out.

'Twang!' The rope goes taut and the bow begins to turn toward the force of the wind. Lawrence opens full throttle and the boat pushes forward, to run parallel to the embankment. Then it swings on an arc of the rope which causes it to turn in a one-hundred-foot radius and to lodge back into the embankment farther up the tracks.

With Lawrence holding the boat in place Tommy

dislodges the anchor and makes his way farther along the track. He hooks the anchor at another rail joint just ahead of the boat and signals to his father. Lawrence releases the boat. 'Twang!' The rope goes taut again and Lawrence is on another arc back to the embankment farther ahead.

It is beginning to rain again. As Tommy staggers toward the next connection, he has an idea. He could increase the distance gained if, instead of placing the anchor at a joint directly in front of the boat he placed the anchor at the next joint fifty feet ahead. He does so and signals his father. Again Lawrence releases the boat and the wind turns it away.

'Twang!' The rope goes taut. However, the tension is not straight from the rail toward the boat but from the rail toward the boat at an angle. 'Zing!' The anchor slides back from next to the joint plate to where the rope's tension is straight to the boat.

As before, Lawrence opens full throttle and the boat pushes forward running parallel to the embankment. 'Zing!' The anchor slips forward with him back toward the joint plate. 'Clank!' Lawrence begins the turn back on the arc toward the embankment.

However, the force of the anchor hook's sliding toward and then hitting the joint plate causes the anchor to rotate, forcing the hook upward and releasing its hold on the rail, while another hook rotates downward just ahead of the joint plate. 'Ping!' The first hook releases! 'Clank!' The second hook engages.

'Zing!' The second anchor hook slides the fifty foot length of rail to the next joint plate. 'Clank!' Lawrence holds the boat parallel to the embankment. But the anchor spins again. 'Ping!' 'Clank!' 'Zing!'

'Clank!' 'Ping!' 'Clank!' 'Zing!'

Tommy sees what is happening and breaks into a run to catch up. Suddenly he is airborne. He floats away from the tracks and down the embankment, landing on his chest inches away from the water. The wind tries to push him into the water but he drags his right arm as a rake to stop his slide.

'Clank!' 'Ping!' 'Clank!' 'Zing!'

Lawrence desperately tries to turn toward shore.

'Clank!' 'Ping!' 'Clank!' 'Zing!'

The fortress is coming into view. How can he stop the anchor?

'Clunk!' The boat turns on the arc toward shore.

The anchor holds. 'Bump!' The boat stops at the embankment directly in front of the fortress. Lawrence takes a deep breath and exhales. "Whew!" Then he notices that the wind is not blowing so hard. The fortress is shielding him from the storm.

With the women still crouched in the bottom of the boat, Lawrence climbs out into the shallow water and pulls the boat further ashore. Then he follows the rope back toward the pinned-down anchor. As he walks out from the shelter of the fortress he is almost knocked over by the wind. He finds the anchor wedged between a rail and a cement slab that was poured to give workmen easy passage across the tracks between train cars and the fortress. That is why the anchor stopped sliding.

Lawrence looks up the tracks to see Tommy, almost half a mile back, struggling toward the fortress. Then he returns to the fortress, pulls tight the rope from the boat, and wraps the anchor end around an angle iron embedded in the cement near the entrance. He returns to the boat and helps Elsie crawl out. "The wind is not blowing hard here. Nevertheless, hold tightly to the rope up to the door."

Next he helps Molly climb out of the boat and guides her by the rope up to the door. He produces a key and unlocks the small door embedded in the larger wooden sliding door. The door initially resists but, with additional pressure, opens inward with ease. Lawrence escorts the two women inside. There are no chairs, only a workbench with some tools. However, a hand rail car is parked in the middle of the floor. Molly and Elsie are happy to sit on its platform.

Lawrence steps back outside and sees Tommy struggling against the wind a short distance from the fortress. Bracing himself, he steps from the shelter of the fortress into the full fury of the wind and hastens as best he can to Tommy. Nearly knocked down by the continuous buffeting, he finally reaches Tommy and, with his body, shields him from the wind. Then they both struggle back to the shelter of the fortress. Once inside, Tommy collapses on the floor. Lawrence slides to the floor with his back to the wall adjacent to the hand rail car. With all four of his family now safely within the confines of the fortress, Lawrence feels secure for the first time since he left his cabin early this morning.

# CHAPTER 19

# BOAT CRISIS

For a long while the four say nothing as they rest like rag dolls draped over furniture, crumpled where they fell, while they slowly regain strength. The wind is outside and harmless. Elsie can feel more than she can hear - a sort of 'wump, wump' as the gusts boil over the fortress.

Finally she raises her head to survey her environment. It seems she is in a large rectangular room with the long side running parallel to the railroad tracks outside. There are only two sources of light. One is on the side they entered, the large windowless sliding door. Embedded within this door is a smaller standard door with a single glass pane window about a foot high and a foot wide. On the opposite side of the room, the storm-facing side, carved into the cement wall, is a single window about four feet high by two feet wide, framed by a metal mullion.

The half of the room in which they sit is lighted by the two windows and contains the handcar and the workbench, above which hang hooks, rope, and chain across the end wall. On the side walls in the corners, rising from the floor to the ceiling, are embedded curved steel rods which form steps for ladders.

The other half of the room looks dark and empty. Elsie can barely make out steel rod ladders rising up the side walls in the corners there also.

As Elsie's eyes grow accustomed to the dark, she sees a large hook hanging overhead above the railroad handcar. The hook is attached to a steel cable that winds around the drum of a hoist which is secured to beams in the ceiling. A long axle extends across the ceiling from the drum to a gear system attached to the wall. A loop of chain is linked to the gears and hangs down the wall next to the wooden sliding door.

Tommy stands up and becomes interested in the tools attached to the wall above the workbench.

He removes several tools, looks them over, and then hangs them back up. Then he reaches toward a small sledgehammer. His first challenge is just to pick up the heavy tool. The more he handles it the bolder he becomes. As he swings the hammer by his side, he loses his grip and the sledgehammer falls to the cement floor with a 'clunk' next to his leg. "Better put that hammer back on the workbench," counsels Lawrence. "The last thing we need now is for one of us to get hurt."

With both hands Tommy lifts the sledgehammer from the floor and places it back on the workbench. He turns and looks out through the open door. A motion catches his eye so he walks to the door for a closer look. Then he turns toward the others and shouts with alarm. "Dad, the boat is loose!"

Lawrence jumps up and runs to the door. The boat is still tethered but is also weaving back and forth in open water, battered by wind gusts sweeping around the fortress. Gripping the rope, Lawrence rushes out toward the boat. Buffeted by wind gusts and bursts of rain, he quickly realizes that the storm is not over.

"How can this happen?" he whispers to himself as

he draws near to the boat, which is only about three feet from shore. "I pulled the boat firmly onshore when we arrived. It is tethered and rope doesn't stretch; but the boat is now floating in the water."

Lawrence wades into a few feet of water to grasp the bow and pull the boat back to land. He beaches the boat as far as he can and walks back to the fortress with an additional four feet of rope in his hand. "How can this happen?" he again whispers to himself. "Perhaps the way I wrapped the rope around the angle iron was not as secure as I thought."

He enters the fortress and addresses his audience. "That boat is our livelihood. It holds our food and fuel. We have to bring it inside the fortress."

He points toward the handcar and exclaims. "This has to go! Molly, you are going to have to move. Tommy, help me move this car outside and put it on the tracks."

He goes to the large sliding door and pushes it open. Then he and Tommy wheel the hand car out of the fortress, coax it over the cement slab, and onto the rails outside. Lawrence pushes the car all the way to the edge of the fortress and lets go. It rolls into the driving wind for a short distance and stops.

"Okay. Let's get the boat in!" exclaims Lawrence.

He unwraps the rope from the angle iron and he and Tommy walk back to the women. "Okay. We are going to play a game of tug-of-war. The boat is heavy when empty. With the food, water and fuel it carries, plus wet burlap bags and rainwater, the boat probably weighs four to five hundred pounds."

He hands the rope to Tommy. "You three pull from this end. I will go back and push the boat from the stern. Hopefully, we can inch the boat up the embankment and into the fortress."

With the large sliding door now open, the sound and vibration of the 'wump, wump' from the wind bursting over the fortress are much stronger. Tommy, Elsie, and Molly pull the rope tight as Lawrence follows it back outside toward the boat. It is now raining heavily. "Just great!" speaks Lawrence to nobody. "All that more water in the boat!"

Putting his safety goggles over his eyes, he wades into knee-deep water at the stern of the boat. The sound of the rain pouring on the bags of food, canteens, and fuel cans is almost deafening. Shouting at the top of his voice, Lawrence begins the cadence, "Pull!" "Pull!" "Pull!" "Pull!" "Pull!"

As they pull with all their might, Molly and the two children fall into sync with Lawrence. The boat inches forward. After about fifteen minutes of pulling, they have the boat far enough out of the water for Lawrence to tip the motor up to lift the propellers out of the water. He opens the drain plug in the back of the boat and allows the accumulated rainwater to pour out.

In another fifteen minutes they have managed to pull/push the boat up the steepest part of the embankment to where the ground levels off to go over the tracks. Finally the boat slides over the cement surface between the rails and the doorway and into the fortress. Lawrence and Tommy struggle to turn and center the boat along the axis of the rectangular room. When at last they finish and declare victory, Elsie notices that the boat rests almost directly beneath the hoist, with its hook hanging down to about ten feet above their heads.

"Whew!" pants Lawrence to catch his breath. "That was tough. Now that the boat is inside we are safe."

He pants some more and smiles at Tommy. Then he turns to Molly. "Molly, I am famished and feel like celebrating. Do you have any snacks that are easily available?"

"Let me see," smiles Molly as she reaches toward one of the burlap bags secured to the boat. "I'm sure I can find something."

CHAPTER 20

# NEW DANGER

Molly opens one of the burlap bags and produces a package of dried beef and some fruit. "Now, with some water, I think this should keep us for awhile"

As Molly assembles the snacks she turns toward Lawrence. "Lawrence, please close the doors; the sound of the storm bothers me."

Lawrence slides the large door shut, then he closes the smaller door. On the outside wind-driven rain sweeps across the handcar. Suddenly the handcar is airborne, swept off the embankment and into the main channel. On the inside the 'wump, wump' sounds fade away, to be replaced by a barely audible 'roar' coming from the direction of the ceiling.

They sit on the boat seats while enjoying their snacks. Because Molly is serving, the order of seating is rearranged. Elsie sits on Molly's seat at the bow. Tommy has relinquished his seat and now sits where Elsie had sat. Molly sits in Tommy's seat.

After lunch, Elsie curls up on the bottom of the boat just under her seat and falls asleep. Tommy comforts himself among the bags of food and does the same. Molly lies down on her back on her seat, using a food bag as a pillow, and drapes her legs over the side of the boat. Lawrence does the same.

Molly dozes off. Sometime later she is jolted awake by a loud 'CRACK.' The roaring of the wind seems to have gotten inside the fortress. Then she feels a cool spot on her arm. Water is dripping from the ceiling. She shifts her position to avoid the water, closes her eyes, and tries to nap.

Unable to fall asleep, Molly opens her eyes. The noise of the wind roaring above the ceiling has deepened almost to the sound of thunder. She is looking at the large hook hanging from the ceiling about ten feet above her. The hook seems to be swaying slowly back and forth like a large pendulum that has been given a nudge.

But more alarming are the shadows on the walls. With all the clouds and rain, not much light is coming through the two windows. It gets even dimmer as she looks higher up the wall toward the ceiling. However, there are shadows on the walls that are seemingly cast by almost ghostlike creatures. Some look like irregular blobs and others like headless creatures with legs. They are barely discernable on a background of slate-gray cement.

She turns toward the large window with the metal mullion. Raindrops splatter against the window and trickle down its face. After watching the window for awhile, she whispers to Lawrence. "Are you awake?"

"Yes, I am awake."

"Look at the window and tell me what you see."

Lawrence studies the window. "I see rain hitting the window."

"Look more closely. Do you notice times when the rain appears heavier?"

"Like now?"

"Yes."

"And now?"

"Yes. What do you think is causing it?"

"Not sure. It could be the wind is ripping off tops of waves and splashing them onto the window."

"Do you think the waves are that high?"

"Don't know. But from the sound of the wind roaring over the roof, the wind is that high. With a beating like this, I wonder how long that window will hold up."

Lawrence sits up and positions himself to be able to step out of the boat easily. Pointing to the hook suspended over his head he says, "There are some hooks and rope over around the workbench. I can fashion some lines for the boat and attach them to the hoist, then lift us up above the window just in case it blows in."

Lawrence steps out of the boat. 'Sploosh!' He looks down to find himself standing in ankle-deep water. With wide eyes he turns back to Molly as he exclaims, "It's flooding in here!"

He sloshes to the door, looks out its window, and turns toward Molly. "It's flooding out there. Yes, the waves are that high. We're in trouble!"

Lawrence looks down into the boat. Water is surging into it through the open drain in the bottom. After he hastily reinserts the plug, he sloshes to the workbench, cuts four equal lengths of rope, and ties a hook on each end of the four tethers. Draping the ropes over his shoulder, he wades to the chain hanging along the wall, which is linked to the overhead hoist. It takes many pulls on the chain to lower the hook just a little, but Lawrence is making progress.

Meanwhile, Molly, sitting on her seat on the boat, watches the water splash against the window. Most of what she hears is the thunderous roar coming down from the ceiling, but occasionally there is a distinct 'splat' of water slamming against the window pane.

Lawrence lowers the hoist hook to about five feet above the boat. That is low enough for him to hang the four tethers on the hook. Then he secures the tethers to the boat by hooking the ropes through eyelet bolts attached to the boat's railing, two near the bow and two at the stern.

He raises the hoist and watches the lines to the boat become taut. Pulling with extra force, he is able to lift the boat. Once lifted free, the hull slides across the floor to center the boat directly under the hoist hook. The shaking wakes up Elsie and Tommy. Their eyes widen as they see Lawrence standing next to the wall pulling the hoist chain. As they sit up he shouts, "Stay low! If the window breaks it will scatter glass all over the boat." Elsie and Tommy crouch down obediently!

Gradually the boat's hull clears the slowly rising waters on the floor of the fortress.

CHAPTER 21

# BROKEN WINDOW

As Lawrence raises the hoist against the full weight of the boat, Molly remains fixed on the window.

'Splat'! 'Splat'! 'Splat'! Wave-augmented water slams against the window. 'Splat'! 'Splat'! 'Chink'! A tiny semicircular crack appears at the base of the window. A small stream of water trickles from the middle of the sill down the interior wall to the water covering the floor.

Molly crouches down.

'Splat'! 'Splat'! 'FOOOM'! The window disintegrates into small glass shards which are blasted across the room in a howling jet of air and water. The mixture explodes over the boat and onto the wall behind it. Ears 'pop' under the jump in air pressure.

'CRASH'! An invisible fist punches through the wood of the sliding door, breaking it into large pieces which vanish outward into the raging storm.

Molly screams! But the sound cannot be heard over the screaming of the wind through the broken window. The wind blasts across the boat, onto the wall behind it, and tries to suck Lawrence out through the empty space left by the sliding door. Hand over hand, he frantically pulls the chain to lift himself safely away from the opening, but the loop of chain, attached to the gears of the hoist, merely pulls down and does not move him at all. His struggle gains him nothing save for lifting the boat a few inches.

A huge wave slams against the side of the fortress. 'FOOOM'! Water blasts through the window, soaking everyone. Ears 'pop' as the wave blocks the wind from blowing through the window, causing the air pressure to drop. Ears 'pop' again as the water level drops and the screaming wind returns.

The wave splits around the outside of the fortress, merges again on the downwind side, and surges back through the opening left by the sliding door. It pushes Lawrence into the fortress away from the door. But simultaneously, the wave lifts the boat and pushes it away from Lawrence.

As the wave collapses, the boat falls with it. The tethers go tight as the water level drops. JERK! Then the receding wave pulls Lawrence toward the opening left by the demolished sliding door.

Hanging from the hoist hook, the boat swings back and forth like a pendulum.

'FOOOM'! Another wave hits the fortress and water slams through the open window. The spray blasts across the boat and tries to drag Lawrence out of the door opening.

Desperately Lawrence clings to the bottom of the loop of chain hanging from the hoist.

'Sloosh'! The back-wave surges through the door opening and drags Lawrence toward the boat again, but also lifts and pushes the boat away. The wave collapses. The boat falls with the wave. JERK! The boat is again left swinging on its tethers.

Lawrence sees an opportunity. Clinging from the hoist chain, he twists his body so that his back is against the wall. He lifts his right leg behind him, extends his left leg forward, and shouts, "Molly!"

Molly, hunched in the bottom of the boat, turns away from facing the window and toward Lawrence. As she sees his physical position, she immediately knows what he is about to do. He studies the swinging boat and at the right moment pushes away from the wall with all his might.

Now on her knees on the bottom of the boat, Molly leans forward, allowing her torso to lean against the side just below shoulder high in order to brace herself against being pulled out. She reaches out and grabs Lawrence's extended left leg. "Tommy! Help me!" she screams.

'FOOOM'! Another wave slams through the open window. The spray of water blasts across the boat, against Molly's back, and up Lawrence's nose.

During the brief lull between the blasting spray and the forceful back-wave, Tommy slides next to Molly and grabs Lawrence's leg.

'Sloosh'! The back-wave surges through the door opening. Tommy and Molly cling to Lawrence's leg as the wave lifts and pushes the boat away, pulling

Lawrence away from the wall. The wave collapses. The boat falls to its tethers. JERK!

The jerk vibrates through Lawrence's body. The boat swings back toward the wall, increasing his leverage. As he swings his right leg up, Tommy releases his grip on Lawrence's left leg and lunges toward the right leg. Both he and Molly pull Lawrence toward the boat.

'FOOOM'! Another wave blasts through the open window across the boat and over Molly and Tommy. They have just a moment to position themselves for maximum strength before they hear the 'slosh' as the back-wave slams under the boat lifting it and pushing it away from the wall again.

The wave collapses and they brace for the jerk as the boat's descent is stopped by the tethers. Then, as the boat swings back toward the wall, Molly and Tommy both pull Lawrence's legs as hard as they can, holding him essentially stationary as the boat swings under him. As the boat slides under his knees, he lowers his legs and locks himself to the boat.

Lawrence is stretched out almost horizontally. The boat now holds some of his weight and he has lost his leverage to operate the hoist. Hand over hand he pulls himself about two feet up the lift chain.

'FOOOM'! Another wave blasts through the open window across the boat, over Molly and Tommy and across Lawrence, pushing him toward the wall. Then, 'slosh,' as the back-wave lifts the boat and pushes it and Lawrence away from the wall.

'Ziiing'! With the boat's being lifted by the wave, Lawrence's weight on the chain is sufficient to lift the hoist. When the wave collapses the boat tethers an inch higher.

'FOOM'! 'Slosh'! 'Ziing'! Jerk!

'FOOM'! 'Slosh'! 'Ziing'! Jerk!

'FOOM'! 'Slosh'! 'Ziing'! Jerk!

Slowly the boat is lifted up above the front of the window.

The water level in the fortress is rising above the window sill, so that the opening for the blasting wind and surging waves is slowly being cut off. Tops of the back-waves also are gradually sheared off by the top of the sliding door opening into the fortress. This reduces the violent rising and falling motion of the boat.

Finally, a gasping Lawrence calls to Tommy.

"Tommy. Can you see the anchor rope lying in the boat?"

"Yes."

"Pick it up in the middle and hold it so that the stretch between you and Mother is long enough for me to grab."

Tommy pulls up a length of rope and hands it to Molly.

"Okay, Mom. On three let's toss the rope to Dad. One, two, three."

The length of rope lands on Lawrence's chest. He releases his hold on the hoist chain and grabs the rope. Tommy and Molly pull back, lifting Lawrence into a sitting position as he slides onto the third seat.

Lawrence struggles back to his stern seat and collapses.

CHAPTER 22

# WINNING THE HOIST

The boat bobs with the wave action within the fortress. Now familiar with the pattern, Molly passes a canteen to a grateful Lawrence and retrieves some dried fruit for him from one of the food bags.

As their battle against raging waves declines, anxiety rises from other problems. Less light filters through the deepening water beneath the boat. The encroaching darkness creates a frightening gloom as the boat bobs up and down among the shadows on the wall, shadows that have grown larger and darker.

Another albeit small source of light is the crack in the ceiling from which water dripped on Molly's arm. Long forgotten during the battle with the waves, now a small waterfall pours incessantly onto the bags of cargo stowed between Elsie and Tommy. The roar of the tempest over the roof filters down through that crack. The winds are not slowing down.

Also there is a periodic rumble that seems to reverberate within the walls of the fortress.

Lawrence sits up slowly. Looking down, he sits with his head in his hands and his elbows on his knees. After a long while, he slowly raises his head. "Tommy. There is a lot of water in the bottom of the boat. Can you bail some of it out?"

"Sure, Dad," replies Tommy, relieved to see his father rejoin the family. He locates the can among the cargo and begins scooping water over the railing.

Molly turns to Lawrence and produces a small smile. "Ready for the next challenge?"

Lawrence stares at her at length. "What?"

"Look up the wall at the shadows. They are darker than they were a while ago."

Lawrence studies the wall. The shadows are only on the wind-facing wall. His eyes widen and his jaw slowly drops. Then he whispers, "That's water seepage!

The storm is blowing through the walls!"

He stares at Molly. Then he turns and tilts his head as if to increase the sensitivity of his hearing.

'Rumble'! 'Rumble'! The cadence superimposes itself on the background howling of the wind above the roof.

'Rumble'! 'Rumble'! Lawrence notices the slow rising and subsiding of the boat relative to the shadows on the wall. The motion of the boat seems to synchronize with the rumbling sound. He turns to Molly. "Do you hear that low rumbling noise?"

"Yes. I hear it. Do you know what it is?"

"Can't be sure. But my best guess is vibration caused by waves hitting the side of the fortress."

"Can the waves knock down the fortress?"

"The fortress was never designed for this. But one thing I know. The deeper the water gets, the stronger the current of the flood is and the greater the leverage of the waves. The fortress sits on a firm foundation. Nevertheless, it's possible that it could be tipped over."

Molly's eyes widen and her jaw slowly drops. Sensing her growing anxiety Lawrence smiles and winks. "But that is the least of our worries."

Molly's facial expression changes. "It seems to me that the deeper the water gets, the less the wall is exposed to waves."

"Yes. Eventually."

'CRACK'! 'SNAP'! A section of the roof breaks and vanishes.

'ROAR'! The violent sound of the wind envelops the fortress. Water streams down inside the downwind wall.

But the loss of part of the roof also increases the light within the fortress so that Lawrence can see the beam from which the hoist hangs. He follows the cable from the hoist down to the large hook which now sways slowly just eighteen inches above their heads. From the hook drop the four tethers that now hang slackly to eyebolts anchored in the railings of the boat.

A scenario plays in Lawrence's mind. *The remaining roof rips off, exposing to the wind the beam that supports the hoist. The anchors that support the beam keep the beam from falling down, not from lifting up. If the wind gets beneath the hoist it could suck it out of the fortress. That would include the cable and the hook that holds the tethers to the boat. The boat could go with it, but more likely one or more of the tethers would snap or one or more of the eyebolts would be pulled out of the railings. That could splinter the wooden sides of the boat. The situation is precarious!*

With no emotion Lawrence stands and carefully steps over the cargo in the bottom of the boat. He steps onto the third seat, grasps the large hook, and detaches the four tether hooks. After lowering three of the tethers into the space between Molly and Tommy, he carefully guides the fourth tether around Molly and the cargo toward his seat at the stern of the boat. He dislodges the tether from the eyebolt at the stern, grasps it in his left hand, and proclaims. "Now let's see if I can snag the hoist chain."

Holding one hook with his left hand, he tosses the tether and its other hook toward the hoist chain.

'Clank'! 'Splash'! The hook hits the wall next to the chain, falls into the water, and goes limp. Lawrence pulls in the tether and tries again.

'Clank'! 'Splash'! Another miss! Lawrence pulls in the tether and tries again.

'Clank'! 'Clink'! 'Splash'! The hook ricochets off the wall, strikes the chain and falls into the water.

Another failure. Lawrence pulls back the limp tether.

Lawrence studies the hoist chain. *Okay, three tries for the chain that pulls the hoist up and three misses. Perhaps I have a better angle toward the chain that pulls the hoist down.*

'Clank'! 'Clink'! 'Splash'! The hook ricochets off the wall, strikes the down-chain, falls into the water and goes limp. Lawrence retrieves the tether.

*Hmmm. Perhaps I can do better if I swing the tether so it strikes the chain higher up.*

'Clank'! 'Clink'! The tether strikes the wall, then slides behind, and hooks onto the down-chain. Lawrence pulls just tight enough to keep the chain hooked while the tether slides down the hoist chain into the water toward the bottom of the loop. Slowly, he pulls the hoist chain up and toward him.

As he pulls the chain toward him, he also pulls the boat toward the wall and out from under the overhanging hoist hook.

Now next to the wall, Lawrence stands and grasps the up-chain. With water pouring down the wall and running down the hoist chain over his hands and over his forearms, he pulls the chain hand over hand. It is a long and tedious job, but the freed hoist hook slowly lifts all the way up to the top of the hoist at the ceiling. He releases the tether hook from the hoist chain and the boat floats free.

With a smile Lawrence slaps water off his hands, sits down, and calls to Molly. "I'm getting hungry. Isn't it time for an afternoon snack?"

## CHAPTER 23

# UNEXPECTED FINISH

Molly reaches toward the bottom of the boat, opens a food bag, and extracts helpings of dried meat and dried fruit. "Come children. Let's have something to eat."

Elsie and Tommy happily join her on the third seat and sit facing Lawrence sitting at the stern. While they savor a much-needed meal, the wave action within the fortress slowly pushes the boat away from the wall and toward the middle of their enclosed pond. The thunderous roar above them doesn't diminish during their family time.

A while after they finish eating Lawrence looks up to notice that the hoist seems closer. He can tell that the boat is floating a little higher.

'CRACK'! 'SNAP'! The remaining section of the roof vanishes. A gust of wind ricochets down the wall and over the boat.

'BANG'! The hoist beam dislodges from its ceiling supports taking the hoist with it!

'SWIIISH'! The hoist chain streaks out of the water, up the wall, and disappears through the top of the fortress.

Lawrence stares at the empty hole above him across which blasts a thunderous roar of air and water. Then, without a word, he reaches down, picks up a bundle of cargo and places it on his seat. Using the bundle as a pillow, he lies down and closes his eyes.

Taking their cue from Lawrence, Molly, Tommy, and Elsie do the same.

A tugging on his shirt awakens Lawrence. The roaring of the wind is all around him. As he looks up from his reclined position all he can see is the roaring jet of air and water streaming just above his face. A sense of disorientation and terror floods his mind. He wrestles with his thoughts. *But wait! I'm still lying on the boat! Where am I?*

He lifts his head and is buffeted by turbulent gusts of spray. He can see the top edges of the walls of the fortress. The flood has continued to rise. With terror he realizes that they are less than four feet from the top of the walls.

Lawrence drops to his hands and knees on the bottom of the boat and crawls over the cargo to the third seat where Molly lies sleeping. He tugs her awake and holds her head so she can't rise up. Then he places his cheek next to her cheek and yells in her ear. "The flood has lifted the boat almost to the top of the fortress walls! Don't sit up or you will be sucked out!"

Molly slides off her seat next to Lawrence. He presses his cheek against her face again and yells, "If the water goes any higher the boat and everything in it will be sucked out! I have to sink the boat!"

Molly nods that she understands what she has been told.

Lawrence yells again. "Stay low here. I am going for Tommy and Elsie!"

He pushes away and slides across the third seat. Tommy is curled up among cargo bags on the bottom of the boat. Lawrence shakes him by the shoulder. Tommy opens his eyes to see Lawrence's face above him and, just above Lawrence, a howling boiling river of spray. He recoils at the sight. "Stay low!" Lawrence screams.

Lawrence pushes past Tommy, slides onto the second seat, and reaches over toward Elsie, who is curled up among cargo bags. He takes hold of her arm and startles her awake. Then he pulls her over the second seat beside him. "Stay low!" he yells, as he lifts her toward the third seat. "Molly is waiting for you!"

Elsie disappears over the third seat, followed quickly by Tommy, who hastens to his knees, crawls to the third seat, and slides over. Then Lawrence picks up the three tethers that had been lying near Tommy and follows over the third seat.

In the sight of all Lawrence reaches over the stern seat and pulls the drain plug. Water surges into the boat. Then he turns to his audience and yells. "I am sinking the boat! This is what we are going to do!"

He grabs one of the tethers and lifts it slightly. "I'm

going to wrap one end of a tether around each of your waists and hook it so it stays! You hold on to the hook on the free end! When the boat goes down, you swim to a corner where there is a ladder in the wall! Hook the free end of your tether to an iron rung as far down as you can reach! Then hang on to the ladder and only allow your face to stick above water!"

With a tether in hand, he reaches toward Elsie. "Elsie! Lie low!"

He slides the tether under her stomach, pulls it around her back, loops it around her again, and wraps the hook around the loops several times to secure it. Finally he hands Elsie the hook attached to the free end of the tether.

Lawrence does the same for Tommy, Molly, and himself. The boat is two thirds full of water by the time he finishes. Molly and the two children are almost submerged. Lawrence yells, "The weight of the motor will cause the stern to sink first! Molly and I will roll off and swim to our assigned corners! Tommy, you and Elsie wait for the bow to sink and then push off! Molly, you and Elsie will take the windward wall! That will offer some protection from the wind! Tommy and I will take the leeward wall! Tommy, you and I are going to be most exposed to the wind! It's going to be rough!"

Lawrence grabs Tommy by the shoulders and pushes him back toward the third seat. He shouts, "Tommy, slide over this seat and the next seat, get low, and wait for the bow to sink! Elsie, you do the same!"

Tommy and Elsie disappear over the third seat. The rising flood is pushing the sinking boat closer to the roaring tempest above their heads. Turbulent gusts slap them down and then try to pick them up again.

The stern sinks. Lawrence and Molly roll off their respective sides of the boat and swim toward the ladders on the walls in their corners of the fortress. In a few seconds water surges over Tommy and Elsie and they can feel the bow dropping away. Then they too roll overboard and start toward their assigned corners.

As she turns toward her corner, Elsie kicks against the side of the bow, forcing it under Tommy's legs and pushing him up above the water's surface. As his calves protrude from the water, an invisible hand seems to grab his ankles and pull him out of the water, flinging him toward the corner of the fortress. As Tommy stretches out his arm to place the tether hook on the iron rung of the ladder in his corner, the invisible hand propels him outward over the fortress wall. Then he is gone!

Lawrence sees it happen! "NOOOOOOO!" he screams.

Drowned out by the roaring of the wind, no one hears his wail. "NOOOOOOO!"

He pulls his tether hook from the iron rung of his ladder and frantically swims toward Tommy's corner. The gale grabs the back of his shirt and tries to pull him out into the storm as well. Feeling the tug, Lawrence lowers his head and pulls himself downward with rapid strokes to safety below the water's surface.

Lawrence swims underwater to Tommy's ladder. Holding tightly to the rungs, he carefully lifts himself to the surface. The wind presses his face against a rung. Groping above, he feels the rope from Tommy's tether. He reaches upward to pull the rope but a thought stops him. *Ripping away the roof may have fractured cement at the top of the wall. If that happened then the rope could be drawn across razor-sharp shards that would cut through the rope if I pull on it.*

He inches his hand up the wall. The wind-driven rain feels like knives stabbing the back of his hand. He slides his hand across the top of the wall. With relief he finds that the wall is not fractured here.

Lawrence pulls on the rope. He has little leverage and the rope does not give. The only way he can get more leverage is to lean out over the wall and pull the rope up. That means exposing himself to the full force of the tempest. He must pull the rope while keeping himself from being sucked out over the wall.

Securing the hook of his own tether to an iron rung, Lawrence climbs further up the ladder. The wind grabs him to pull him over but his tether won't permit that. Instantly, the wind rips his shirt off, exposing his back to the driving rain. The water drops lashing his back feel more like grains of sand, and searing pain shoots over his back and up the back of his neck. Something is trying to pull his hair out by the roots!

Anchoring his toes under an iron rung, Lawrence grabs Tommy's rope, wrenches his body back inside the top of the wall, and ducks under water to shield his body from more pain. As the pain fades away, he lifts his head above water to breathe, gasping as it is difficult to distinguish the boundary between water and air.

He has pulled about a foot of Tommy's tether back inside the wall giving him enough slack to lower its hook down the ladder by one rung.

After catching his breath, he reaches over the wall again. Pain immediately shoots across his back and neck. Nevertheless, he pulls back an additional foot of rope and, as quickly as he can, sinks below the surface to escape the lashing rain. He places the tether hook an additional one rung lower.

Now panting, Lawrence reaches over the wall and retrieves more rope. *Odd,* he thinks. *The pain isn't so bad this time. I guess I've been beaten numb.*

Lawrence climbs the ladder again. The wind tries in vain to pull him over the wall. It seems as if it isn't raining so hard. "What's happening?" he hollers.

He pulls rope until the tether goes taut. Then, for cover, he slips back down the wall into the water. When he resurfaces the roaring is not so loud. It's easier to breathe. "What's happening?" he hollers again.

Now emboldened, he climbs higher up the ladder. Reaching over the top he can feel Tommy's body next to the wall. He positions to pull Tommy back over the wall but a thought stops him. *Tommy is on the leeward side of the wall. I am on the windward side. The storm is worse on my side. Besides, the wind is still too strong to pull him over.*

With the rain beating against his back, Lawrence feels along Tommy's body until he finds his neck. Then he lifts Tommy's head up against the wall so that he can breathe easier.

Using the pain on his back as a gauge, Lawrence can tell that the wind-driven rain is gradually slacking. He holds Tommy's head up until he is certain he can lift him over the wall. Then he grabs an arm just under the shoulder and a leg just under the knee and rolls Tommy up over the wall and into the water in front of him.

"Cough, cough, cough!"

Using his body to shield Tommy from the wind and rain, Lawrence screams. "Tommy, Tommy! I thought we had lost you!"

"Cough, cough!"

"Oh my God!" squeals Lawrence as he draws Tommy into a bone-bruising hug as he stands behind him, using his own body as a shield against the diminishing wind and rain.

After awhile the rain stops. It is still breezy and wavelets are breaking over the wall. Framed by dark clouds scurrying above and the water below, a growing area of brightness is spreading across the waves. “Waaahoooo!” yells Lawrence. “The storm is stopping!”

Finally, the wind decreases to a breeze. Releasing his own tether, he climbs up, stands on the top of the wall, and spreads his arms. “It’s stopping! The storm is stopping!”

Then he falls backward and splashes into the pool framed by the walls of the fortress.

CHAPTER 24

# END OF BRIGHTNESS

After spending hours being exposed to the gloom of imprisonment within the confines of the fortress, the brightness of the clearing skies is almost unbearable. Lawrence regains his composure, swims back to Tommy, and turns to call the others. "Everybody bring me your tethers. I'm going to get the boat!"

Molly and Elsie swim toward Lawrence as he disconnects Tommy's tether and his own. The three hang on to the ladders as Lawrence takes their tethers and dives downward out of sight.

Molly hugs Tommy. "Are you alright?"

Tommy replies with a lethargic "I think so."

"What happened?"

"The wind grabbed me just as I was hooking my tether to the ladder. It pulled me over and, thanks to the tether, I landed outside almost next to the wall. I think the wall protected me. Still it was hard to breathe with all the spray. Then this shirt landed on my face and it helped filter out the water and made it easier to breathe. I stuffed it down my pants when Dad pulled me back."

Tommy reaches into his pants and pulls out Lawrence's shirt. Molly laughs. Then she takes the shirt from Tommy. "I think I know where this shirt belongs."

Tommy continues. "When I felt Dad pulling on the rope I knew I would be safe. He pulled me back to the wall where the storm wasn't so bad"

Molly hugs Tommy again.

'Sploosh'! Lawrence appears in the middle of the pool gasping. "Attached two tethers. Now for the other two."

'Sploosh'! He disappears.

Molly and the children huddle in the corner. The dark storm clouds have vanished. It is still cloudy but it looks as if breaks are forming. The wind is just a light breeze. "Hey," she says. "Let's sit on the wall."

She climbs the ladder and props herself on top of the wall. Elsie comes next followed by Tommy. The three of them look on as a gasping Lawrence surfaces toward the end of the pool. "There! I've got all four tethers hooked up. Now to raise the boat!"

"What are you doing?" queries Molly.

"I hooked the tethers to the boat and ran them to the rungs of the ladders at the four corners. To raise the boat, all I have to do is raise the tethers at the ladders."

After a few more breaths he disappears. In awhile Molly and the children notice the shadow of a boat appearing from the depths of the fortress.

Finally, Lawrence hooks all the tethers to the highest rungs of the four corner ladders. The boat is in the middle of the pool just inches under water. Smiling, he calls out, "Okay you three. Get in the water and come over here. I need you to lift the boat enough so I can bail it out."

He reaches into the boat and grabs the bailing can. As the others arrive, he gives his orders. "Molly, you push up from the bow. Tommy and Elsie, get on opposite sides about halfway down and grab hold of the railing. I will push from the motor."

They take their positions. "Okay. Kick as hard as you can!"

They kick for a few minutes. Nothing happens. "Kick harder! Kick as hard as you can!"

The boat slowly rises, maybe half an inch. "That's it! Keep kicking!"

After several more minutes of kicking the boat has risen maybe another half an inch. Now gasping, Molly calls out. "It isn't working!"

"Oh, but it is!" replies Lawrence. "Keep kicking!"

The boat has risen another inch. Molly stops. "I can't kick anymore!"

Lawrence reaches into the back and replaces the drain plug.

"What were you doing?" Molly scolds.

"Letting water drain out of the boat. You all let go and go back to the wall."

As they let go, the front of the boat sinks back slightly, causing the water to shift forward and allowing Lawrence to lift the stern a few inches. He keeps kicking to keep it above water. Holding the motor by one hand and kicking, he reaches the bailing can into the back of the boat and scoops out water.

Eventually the boat is about four inches out of the water. Exhausted, Lawrence stops bailing and tosses the can toward the front of the boat. He swims to the wall opposite his audience and detaches the tethers. Then he swims back to the boat and pushes it toward the wall.

Lawrence looks up to Tommy. "Tommy, it's your turn. Jump in between the first and second seats and bail. Stay away from the back until you have gotten enough water out so the boat won't swamp."

Tommy steps down into the boat while Lawrence climbs the ladder to join Molly and Elsie.

Patches of blue slice through the remaining clouds. Tommy finishes bailing the boat and the four passengers take their places. A smiling Lawrence addresses his wife. "Molly, I think it's time for a celebration. Break out the dessert. Let's have some of that chocolate!"

Molly gratefully obliges. She opens one of the waterproof cargo bags and pulls out several packages of Hershey's best. They finish the delights just as fatigue sets in. After all that he has done, Lawrence is finished. Tommy is also vanquished but for different reasons. For Molly and Elsie, having endured the incessant roaring of the wind while clinging to the rungs of the ladders was exhausting. They go back to their private places on the boat, rearrange the furniture, and fall fast asleep.

The sun comes out. First it keeps everyone cool by evaporating water from their wet clothes. Having done that, it makes them hot.

Elsie awakens and sits up. As the fog of sleep dissipates, her mind wanders, bringing up a swarm of memories. *She sits in the coach of the Laketon to Fletcher Camp Nine train looking at a massive cement structure in front of which stand workmen, who clamber aboard her car. Stands of mangrove trees welcome her. Streets lined with ordered rows of tent cabins and weathered wooden buildings pass by. A giant alligator thrashes the water. Molly stands guard on the dock with shotgun in hand as she and Tommy frolic in the water. She and Tommy float on a raft suspended in the middle of a pond surrounded by tall grass.*

Now seemingly transported into another world, she sits in a boat that floats on an endless sea but confined to the pool framed by the remnants of the fortress. There are no grasses, no buildings, no mangrove trees, nothing.

The sky is clear and blue. Yet it isn't. There are clouds along the horizon. Rows of clouds. Strangely, save for shadows cast by the early-afternoon sun, no matter which way she looks all the clouds look the same. Now, instead of their being surrounded by grass which looks the same no matter which way one looks, they are surrounded by clouds which look the same all the way to the distant horizon.

Having grown bored with her surroundings, Elsie retreats to her resting place in the front of the boat. As it is now hot, she cannot sleep. At least that's what she thinks, but suddenly she feels cooler. Sitting up she surveys her environment. A light breeze is blowing. Wavelets sparkle in the sunlight.

One of the skills Elsie has gained during her six-week stay on Lungraun's Island is the ability to tell time by the angle of the sun. It looks to be about mid-afternoon. She can also use the sun angle to estimate direction. It seems the wind is blowing from the southwest, not the direction the wind was blowing from when the storm ended.

The clouds have also changed. The clouds in the north seem more distant while the clouds in the south are closer. And there is something strange about those clouds. Usually the closest clouds always seem to be moving faster than the more distant clouds. But these clouds are just the opposite. The distant clouds seem to be moving faster than the closer clouds.

Elsie shakes Tommy's arm to awaken him and whispers, "Tommy. Get up and see. The storm is back."

Tommy looks at her as the wind fluffs her hair. With that incentive, he pulls himself up quickly and sits by her. "Look!" she says as she points toward the south.

Now the clouds are closer. As Tommy looks toward where Elsie points he sees a bank of ragged low-hanging clouds below which the sky is ominously dark. He studies these clouds. "Looks really bad over there. But it's not coming this way."

"I've been watching it," counters Elsie. "The clouds go that way but the storm comes closer."

"That can't be," replies a puzzled Tommy.

"It's like it's on some kind of wheel," answers Elsie.

Tommy shakes Lawrence's arm. "Dad! Wake up! The storm is back!"

Lawrence opens his eyes and looks at Tommy. He need look no further. Above Tommy scurry the low-hanging ragged clouds. He sits up, takes a deep breath, exhales with a sigh, and then commands. "Okay, let's get tethered!"

He reaches behind him and pulls out the drain plug. Water starts filling the boat. "Elsie, you go to the storm-facing corner. Molly, take that corner. Tommy, you and I will take this side. Molly and Elsie, keep your hair in the water so the wind can't pull it out!"

Now tethered, Elsie departs the boat and swims toward her assigned ladder. She climbs the ladder and looks over the wall. Whitecaps splash against it.

It is starting to rain.

## CHAPTER 25

# FALL OF THE FORTRESS

'Raasp'! Lawrence is startled awake by a foreign sound. Then a faint 'gurgling' sound slowly lulls him back to sleep.

'Raasp'! The sound startles him awake again. The 'gurgling sound is louder. He opens his eyes and looks up along the walls through the rectangular hole that was once the roof of the fortress.

The sky is brilliant blue and daylight rains down into the depths of the fortress. Despite the strange sounds all seems at peace. Nevertheless Lawrence, now disoriented, is submerged in thought. *The top of the fortress is 'there.' But shouldn't it be over 'there'?*

Then he remembers. *The winds had increased to*

*a whistle and spray was blowing over the walls when I last saw the boat just inches from sinking. Then the rains became torrential and the winds increased to a loud roar and I was forced to face the wall as wind-driven spray slammed against the back of my head.*

*Now accustomed to the roar of wind-driven spray just overhead, I perceived that it was getting darker. The storm did not increase in ferocity so I figured that it was getting on toward evening. I also noticed that my head was further out of water. That was when I saw that the next rung down on the ladder was visible. The flood was receding.*

*I disconnected my tether, swam to Tommy, helped him down a rung, and freed him from his tether. Then I swam to Elsie and to Molly. I swam with the tethers to the floor of the fortress and attached them to the boat and to the ladders as I had done when the storm had ended. Then I raised the tethers rung by rung until I had lifted the boat to where it came to rest about a foot under water.*

*Now it was almost totally dark. I began with Molly. I guided her from her ladder to swim over and into the boat without exposing her body to the sucking force of the winds. Then I did the same for Tommy and Elsie.*

*As the flood receded and the boat was held by the tethers, the boat gradually drained of water until it was able to float. I plugged the drain and vigorously bailed out the remaining water, allowing the boat to float higher. I disconnected the two tethers at the stern, and doing so allowed the boat to float toward the opposite wall. Then I called to Tommy to disconnect the two tethers next to him and the boat floated free in the middle of its rectangular pool.*

*It was night, the rain stopped, and the wind diminished to a raging howl. Surrounded by cement walls and safely below the open roof, we found our comfort among the cargo bags and fell asleep.*

Lawrence studies the rectangle of daylight above him. A small puff of cloud comes into view. 'Raasp'! The cloud jerks out of view. He suddenly understands why he is so disoriented. The fortress is tipping over!

The waters recede below a narrow gap created by the top of the missing sliding door. Lawrence looks through the gap to assess what is happening. Outside the railroad track has been upended and is pressed against the opening. Escape through the doorway is not possible. Part of that flood is eroding the roadbed and undercutting the foundation of the fortress.

'Raasp'! The fortress tips and sinks further. The current sweeps into the fortress and pushes the boat against the east wall in front of the gap where the window had blown in.

'Bump'! The jolt awakens Molly and the two children. "What's happening?" Molly screams.

"Erosion is tipping over the fortress!"

Lawrence grabs the boat's anchor with its 100 foot length of rope, steps from seat to seat past the bewildered passengers, then to the bow, and jumps into now waist-deep water. He wades to the ladder at the southeast corner next to the south wall and climbs as fast as he can.

Reaching the top he unfurls the rope and allows the anchor to hang outside the south end of the fortress just above the water. Then he swings the anchor back and forth as far as he can and hurls it back toward the nearby upended rails.

'Clank'! The anchor falls across the rails. Lawrence pulls the rope tight and calls. "Tommy. Climb up here and sit on the ledge."

Tommy half dives toward the ladder and hastens

up to the top. Lawrence instructs. "Hang down outside and grab hold of the rope. I will lower you to the water and you can wade to shore by the track."

Tommy obeys. Lawrence lowers him into the water. It is about chest deep. Hanging onto the rope, Tommy pulls himself to shore. He steps up the badly washed out roadbed toward the anchor.

Lawrence calls down to him. "Pick up the anchor and carry it further down the tracks to a safer place beyond the fortress. I will lead out the rope as far as I can."

Tommy picks up the anchor and starts down the tracks. Lawrence holds back enough rope to leave slack for the boat. Then he holds the rest of the rope while Tommy pulls the line until it goes taut and he stops. Lawrence calls out. "Find a place where you can tie down the anchor securely."

Lawrence turns back into the fortress. "Okay, Elsie. It's your turn."

She scrambles up the ladder and sits on the edge of the wall. Lawrence instructs. "Lean out over the wall and grab the rope and I will lower you to the water."

Elsie grabs the rope and Lawrence lowers her down.

She hangs onto the rope until she reaches water that is shallow enough for her to stand. Then she wades to shore and stands near Tommy.

'Raasp'! The top of the wall drops further. It is easier to walk on the wall than on the floor. Water surges back through the window opening, causing the boat to rock violently. "Okay, Molly. Your turn."

Molly waits for the rocking to subside, then abandons ship and climbs the ladder. As she sits on the wall, Lawrence instructs. "Hang over and grab the rope and I will lower you into the water."

"Oh, please," replies Molly. "There is no current here, the water doesn't look that deep, and I know how to swim."

She slides off the wall and falls about ten feet. 'Sploosh.' Then she swims gracefully beside the rope until the water is shallow enough to wade to shore.

'Raasp'! The wall drops again. Following the rope Lawrence walks down the wall back to the boat. He unties some of the straps holding bags of cargo to the bed of the boat. Then he carries several bags to the top of the wall. His original plan was to attach the bags to the rope and let them slide down from the top of the wall to waiting hands. However, the fortress is sinking away from shore and the top is now too low to the water for his plan to work.

He calls out to Molly. "Hey, I need help getting these bags to shore."

Molly, Tommy, and Elsie return to the side of the sinking fortress and form a human chain with Molly being the one wading into the deepest water. They wade out toward Lawrence as far as they can. He is able to toss the bags to Molly who, in turn, tosses them to Tommy, who tosses them to Elsie, who stows them on shore.

The strategy works until Lawrence comes to the gas cans. These are too heavy to toss to Molly. Lawrence secures two tethers, links them together and to the gas cans, then tosses the free end of the tethers to Molly and lowers the cans into the water so that Molly can pull the cans to shore.

Finally, the boat is empty except for the motor and Lawrence. He returns to the boat and waits.

'Raasp'! The fortress sinks further. The top of the wall settles below the water level. Wavelets wash in and surround the boat. Lawrence climbs out of the boat to assess the depth of the water. It is only about an inch deep, too shallow to push the boat through. He returns to the boat to wait.

Meanwhile, Molly and the children carry the bags of cargo from the washed out area down the roadbed to where Tommy had secured the rope and anchor. She sorts the bags and opens those containing the groceries she had procured from the FC9 market. One of the bags contains a tarp, which she unwraps and lays out on the slope of the railroad embankment. Then she spreads out the booty to assess how much food is left.

'Raasp'! The fortress subsides some more. More water rushes through the gap that was once the roof. The flow is deep enough for Lawrence to push the boat through. Just as the stern drops into open water, he jumps into the back. The boat floats free.

As the current pulls him away from the fortress toward open water, the anchor rope goes taut and turns the boat to face the tracks.

'Twang'! The rope slides across the sandy embankment and throws sand on Molly and the two children. As they look toward the water, Lawrence calls, "Hey, you three. How about pulling me in?"

# CHAPTER 26

# TENSE MOMENT

Molly tends to the foodstuffs spread out on the tarp while Tommy and Elsie take charge of pulling in the boat. At first they pull the rope hand over hand, but once they have retrieved enough rope, they put the rope over their shoulders and walk up the roadbed. After a few minutes the boat bumps ashore.

Lawrence drags the bow of the boat onto the sand. Then he turns and gives Molly a giant hug. Tommy and Elsie close in and he draws them into the hug as well. Looking beyond Molly along the washed out roadbed, turned up tracks, and the exposed walls of the fortress, which lies mostly underwater, he takes a deep breath and sighs. “We made it!”

He pauses for a moment and finishes, “…for now!”

Molly looks up at him with a puzzled expression. “What do you mean?”

“I have no idea how far up the tracks the destruction goes. If the washouts go far, it will take weeks to repair the roadbed. How much food do we have?”

“I packed enough food for three days. Yesterday was a half a day and…”

Molly looks up to the sky. “…judging from the sun angle it is now approaching noon. Nobody has eaten anything yet or had any water. That means we have to stop and eat something. That’s another half day. So, after today, we will have food for two days.”

Lawrence raises his hand and strokes his chin and confirms. “We will have enough food for two days, maybe a little more if we ration.”

“Will that be enough to get to help?”

“Depends on where help will be. There won’t be enough gas to get the boat back all the way to Laketon. Given that the flood is still receding, we will face a current much of the way.”

“How far is Laketon?”

"About fifty miles."

"Well, when can we leave?"

"Not today. The currents are still too strong and the water is too high to get safely back under the bridge. Besides, I must strip down the motor, wash off any saltwater, oil the parts, and reassemble it. That will take the remainder of today."

"That means if we leave tomorrow morning we will leave with two days of food."

Lawrence twists his lips. "How about water?"

"We brought four large canteens. Two are full. The third is a little less than half full. The fourth is empty"

"Hmmm," ponders Lawrence. "I have two full cans of gas and one nearly empty. Against a current, that could take us probably twenty miles over probably a full day."

"That leaves another thirty miles to walk with the last day of food."

"Yes. If we carry what we need and walk at two miles per hour for ten hours, we can make twenty miles per day. At that rate, it will take at least a day and a half to get to Laketon."

Molly looks grim. "Okay, let's plan for that. The

children will likely need the most food. Water could be our problem."

Molly turns toward Tommy and Elsie. "Children, it's time to eat. We have dried meat, dried fruit, water, and chocolate."

They all take their places on the tarp as Molly passes out foodstuffs. "Please enjoy your menu because this is all we have to eat for the remainder of our trip," she smiles.

Silence surrounds the tarp as they all devour Molly's offerings.

As they finish, Lawrence draws their attention. "This afternoon would be a good time for everyone to get rest. I am going to strip the motor so will need the tarp."

Molly cleans up and repacks the food bags. Tommy and Elsie retreat to sit on some exposed railroad ties. Lawrence pulls the boat back into the water, turns it around, and drags it back on shore stern first. He walks to the stash of cargo bags, locates one of his, opens it, and extracts a tool box and a can of oil. On his way back to the boat he picks up the half-used water canteen.

Setting his loot on the edge of the tarp, he returns to the boat and locates the bailing can. He fills the bailing can with fresh water from the canteen and then sits down on the tarp for a brief rest.

Bored, Tommy and Elsie walk down the tracks away from the fortress. They balance themselves on rails left suspended above washouts. Finally, they come to a place where the washouts are so extensive the tracks disappear under water.

"Looks like this is as far as we can go," comments Tommy. "Let's go back."

They reverse their path and head back toward their encampment.

Meanwhile, Lawrence opens his toolbox and extracts a crescent wrench. He loosens the bracket that holds the motor to the boat and hauls the motor to the tarp. He removes the metal cover, exposing the mechanical workings of the motor. Each nut, bolt, or object that is small enough goes into the fresh water bath contained in the bailing can.

As it approaches late afternoon, some clouds block the searing sun and provide relief to those exposed on the railroad roadbed. The boat motor, reduced to component parts, lies on the tarp. Lawrence washes each part in fresh water and wipes it with an oil-soaked rag.

Tommy and Elsie return and are sternly warned to keep away from the tarp. They depart and stroll slowly down the roadbed the other way toward the fortress.

Once he has cleaned and oiled each part, Lawrence begins the job of reassembling his motor. Molly approaches and queries. "Are you going to finish by suppertime?"

A rough skeleton of the motor takes shape. "Give me half an hour." Lawrence replies.

Molly sits down at the edge of the tarp and watches. Finally Lawrence smiles. "It's satisfying to see that all of the nuts and bolts are used up!"

He stands and, with effort, picks up the motor and lugs it back to the boat, where he reattaches it to the holding bracket on the stern.

He walks past Molly, picks up one of the full gas cans, and walks back to his newly assembled motor. "Now to see if it runs."

Lawrence places the gas can in the back of the boat and connects the fuel line to the motor. Pushing the boat out as far as the anchor rope will allow, he lowers the props into the water, inserts the starter key, and pulls the crank.

'Crank'! Nothing happens.

'Crank'! 'Crank'! The boat sits silently. Molly looks on apprehensively. Lawrence consoles, "It will take a few cranks to get gas down the fuel line."

'Crank'! 'Crank'! 'Crank'! 'Crank'!

'Crank'! 'Put, put.'

'Crank'! 'Put, put, sputter, put, put, varoom'!

Taking a deep breath, Molly utters a sigh of relief.

## CHAPTER 27

# FRESH START

The next morning they are awakened by daylight and calling birds. Molly takes a deep breath and sighs. “I guess its time for breakfast.”

Lawrence sits up and surveys his surroundings. “Kinda comforting that we had a night when nothing changed.”

Molly lays out the breakfast fare. “Eat up everybody. Same menu as yesterday.”

After they finish eating, Molly cleans up what little needs to be packed up and folds the tarp. Lawrence notices that Elsie climbs the embankment, crosses the tracks, and disappears on the opposite side. Tommy follows her.

“Tommy!” Lawrence calls out. “Come over here and give me a hand. Help me carry the cargo back to the boat.”

The embankment is cleared and the boat quickly loaded. Everyone gathers by the boat. Lawrence proclaims, “Okay, we are going to seat ourselves in the usual manner. Molly, take the seat at the bow. Then Elsie take seat two, and Tommy has seat three. Of course I have the stern.”

Elsie and Tommy clamber aboard. Lawrence retrieves the anchor and coils the rope. “Oh. Wait a minute,” Molly proclaims.

She turns and walks up the embankment and disappears over the other side. Lawrence wades beside the boat, places the anchor and its rope in the space between seats three and four, and climbs aboard.

Molly reappears. She takes hold of the bow, pushes the boat free, and climbs aboard. The boat slowly floats backward in silence while Lawrence inserts the starter key in the motor.

‘Crank’! ‘Put, put, sputter, put, put, varoom’!

‘Varoom, put, put, varoom’! Lawrence tests the motor to be sure it is ready for full power. Then, ‘click’, he sets the motor for reverse and pulls back in an arc to clear the shore and to point the boat toward deeper water. 'Click.' Lawrence sets the motor for forward, and the boat moves toward the main channel, slowly at first, as they take a long departing look at the place where they camped overnight. They approach the fortress with a sense of awe.

It all seems so quiet and serene. They glide past the mostly submerged fortress and position for the turn into the channel that goes under the bridge. With all of the surrounding soil washed away, the bridge stands naked on its supports. There never was much space underneath it and the water is still running high.

Lawrence turns toward the bridge into the current. The network of iron girders looms ominously overhead and they have to duck as they pass underneath it. Once they have cleared the bridge, Lawrence turns north into the canal that runs parallel to the railroad tracks. They are headed toward Laketon.

Elsie looks around Molly and up the canal ahead. It disappears over the horizon. Lawrence guides the boat slowly in order to conserve gas.

The adjacent railroad tracks are a continuous

display of desolation. Large washouts leave the tracks hanging over emptiness. In other areas the tracks have been overturned and uplifted so they stand on edge, somewhat like spines down the back of a dinosaur. Lawrence stares at one such turned-up track then announces, "Looks like these tracks were lifted out when the flood came in."

By midmorning no upturned tracks are visible. There are washouts, but they are fewer in number and not so deep. Lawrence comments, "I would guess we have gone about five miles. There used to be grass on this side of the canal. Now there is just open water."

Time seems to freeze. The monotony of the canal, the nearby railroad embankment, and the adjacent waters forces Elsie to search for small changes. They pass a few isolated stands of broken-over grass. Then more stands of broken-over grass.

'Put.' 'Put.' 'Sputter.' The boat motor shuts down and the boat quickly drifts to a stop. Lawrence tips the motor forward revealing grass tangled around the propeller. He pulls the grass from the propeller and tips the motor shaft back into the water.

'Crank!' 'Put, put, varoom.' The motor pushes the

boat forward up the canal again but not for long.

'Put.' 'Put.' 'Sputter.' The boat stops again. "More grass tangled around the propeller," grumbles Lawrence.

Molly stands up and looks into the water. "There's grass all over, just under the surface. The flood must have washed it into the canal."

"It looks like something is floating on the surface up ahead," adds Elsie.

Molly turns and looks up the canal. "Yes, there is a mass of floating grass up there."

Lawrence studies Molly. Then he clears the grass from the propeller, returns it into the water, and starts the motor. 'Put, put, varoom.'

'Click.' He puts the motor in 'forward' and turns to maximum speed.

'Roar!' The boat lurches forward but not very fast. Lawrence looks down to see chopped pieces of grass boiling up behind the boat.

For the next quarter mile, they grind through mats of floating grass. Finally, the boat speeds up and Lawrence slows the motor. Somewhat wistfully he declares, "Looks like we are through the grass but we used up a lot of fuel."

As morning grades into afternoon some clouds provide relief from exposure to the direct sunlight. The canal is free of mats of floating grass. They are passing stands of grass that are not broken-over.

The clouds have thickened and Molly hears a rumble of thunder directly overhead. She calls to Lawrence. "Stop the boat!"

Lawrence shuts down the motor just as large drops of rain splash into the canal. Molly rummages through the food bags at her feet and produces the tarp. "Quick, Tommy! Hand me the empty water canteens!"

Tommy passes up two empty canteens. Molly unrolls the tarp and hands one end to Elsie. "Here, pass this back to Lawrence. Everyone, hold the tarp over your heads."

She sets an opened canteen on Elsie's seat as the rain beats down on the tarp with a 'roar.' "Lawrence, hold your end high. Let's direct the water toward Elsie and refill the canteens."

The deluge lasts for about ten minutes and then tapers off to a light drizzle. The canteens are filled and Molly refolds the tarp. Lawrence starts the motor and the scenery of standing grass slowly passes by again.

A gap in the grassy wall opens into a side channel. Elsie is captivated by an orange-red ball hanging exactly halfway between the ground and the base of distant remnants of rain clouds.

Lawrence reduces the power of the motor and turns the boat toward the railroad embankment. Expressing a small smile he proclaims. "Looks like its time to finish up for the day. I'm pulling over so we can all get out and stretch. The other side of the tracks is private."

Molly sets up the tarp on flat ground near the tracks and spreads four places of food – dry meat, dry fruit, chocolate, and water. On a rail facing the setting sun Lawrence, Molly, Tommy, and Elsie sit like statues.

After the sun falls below the horizon and they are enveloped in twilight, Elsie senses a strange feeling of aloneness. Not that she is alone or lonely; she is surrounded by the closest of family. It's just that the rest of the world has vanished. It seems that they are the only people left.

As darkness settles in, Lawrence proclaims, "I think we should move back into the boat. Snakes or gators could come by and crawl up on the bank sometime during the night. I will anchor us in the middle of the canal. Besides, we are used to sleeping in the boat."

CHAPTER 28

# RESCUE

'Put, put, sputter, sputter.' The boat motor goes silent. "Well, we knew this was going to happen," mumbles Lawrence. "So, it has happened. We are out of fuel."

He steers the slowing boat toward the railroad embankment and throws the anchor onshore. "We walk from here."

Lawrence pulls the stern toward shore so that the side of the boat rests against the embankment. "Okay, everybody out. Molly, what's our food situation?"

"I checked that out after breakfast. We have enough food to last us today and through noon tomorrow. Maybe tomorrow night if we go easier. Water is okay thanks to yesterday's rainstorm. We still have three full canteens"

Lawrence climbs out of the boat. "We will only take our food and water and anything else that's necessary for our hike. It's still a long way to Laketon."

"I will bring the tarp," replies Molly. "It may come in handy if there is another rain."

"Okay," replies Lawrence. "I will carry two canteens. Tommy, you carry the third canteen. Molly gets the two remaining grocery bags and Elsie, you carry the tarp."

Lawrence presses the anchor into the sand next to a railroad tie. Then he straps the two canteens across his shoulders. "Tommy, you and Elsie go ahead and we will follow. You two will set the pace. It's the easiest to walk down the ties between the rails."

Tommy and Elsie start walking along the tracks. Lawrence assists Molly in strapping the grocery bags across her back. He smiles broadly. "At least we won't have to worry about trains coming up from behind us."

They walk for several hours. Then Lawrence calls out. "Hey everybody, I think it's time for a lunch break."

Molly lowers her bags next to the rail facing the canal. The others put down their loads and gather around her. Molly smiles with a bit of a giggle. "Dried meat, dried fruit, and water. Enjoy!"

"No chocolate?" questions Tommy.

"Out of chocolate," answers Molly.

Elsie sits on the rail facing the canal. As she looks across the canal toward the grass wall, she notices that the grass is growing from soil, not water.

It is getting hot. A light breeze is blowing but it doesn't help much. Elsie studies the sky. A few white puffy clouds are scattered across a deep blue sea, not the big storm clouds that provided the shade of yesterday.

After they finish eating and rest for about half an hour, Lawrence gives the command. "Okay, let's load up and get going."

The loads they are carrying seem a little heavier. Tommy and Elsie walk ahead. They do not talk. Perhaps it is to conserve energy. Perhaps there is nothing to say. After awhile, Elsie is overcome by the feeling that she is walking but not going anywhere. The scenery doesn't change.

'Ping!'

"Hey, Dad," Tommy calls back. "What was that noise?"

"That 'pinging' sound?"

"Yes."

"It's called 'rail sing.'"

"What causes it?"

Could be a number of causes. Could be caused by expansion of the rails in the heat. Sometimes distant trains cause the rails to sing."

"You mean there is a train coming?" queries Molly with eyebrows raised.

"Most likely heat expansion."

Elsie studies the tracks that go to the horizon. "It seems that the sky is a little darker over the tracks."

"It could be an optical illusion," follows Tommy.

The back of Lawrence's shirt becomes wet and perspiration forms across his brow. Tommy's shoulders droop. Let's take a water break proclaims Lawrence."

They finish half of the water in Tommy's canteen. So, at least, his load is lighter.

'Ping.'

They climb back on the tracks. "I still think the sky

is darker over the tracks," proclaims Elsie.

"Maybe you are right," answers Lawrence as he studies the horizon.

Molly looks down the tracks but says nothing.

After they have walked awhile, Elsie, emboldened by Lawrence's agreement with her observation, calls back. "The darkness is not directly over the tracks. It seems to be shifted to the side a little."

Lawrence agrees. "And given the wind direction, it could be a plume of smoke."

They stand, looking down the tracks. A tiny black dot appears on the horizon directly ahead. "Yes," proclaims Lawrence. "I do believe there's a train coming!"

Molly inhales deeply, exhales a sigh, and closes her eyes.

The black dot grows larger and takes shape. The darkness is clearly the smoke plume from a locomotive. Lawrence drops his two canteens, steps in front of Tommy and Elsie, and waves broadly with both arms. The smoke plume shrinks then almost disappears.

The train is still approaching but slowing. Brakes squeal as it grinds to a stop about one hundred feet in front of them.

'Toot!' 'Toot!' 'Toot!'

Lawrence, followed by the family, walks slowly toward the hissing locomotive. Three men descend from one side of a passenger coach and carefully thread their way along side the train while trying not to slip off the edge of the embankment.

Lawrence recognizes the three men. The first is supervisor Stan Faulkner, the manager for railroad construction. A tall muscular man with graying hair, yet with physical stature sufficient to gain the respect of any man, he approaches with his mouth and brow set in a stern expression. Then his mouth cracks into a broad smile as he grabs Lawrence by his shoulders and shakes him. "Man, am I glad to see you!"

Lawrence smiles as Faulkner releases his grip and extends a hand toward Molly's shoulder. "Molly! Children!"

He turns back to Lawrence. "I'm bringing a work crew of forty men to repopulate FC9 and to look for you."

"What have you brought with you?"

"A coach and a car with supplies and tools."

“Not enough. There are major washouts down there. You will need at least a dozen cars loaded with fill and a crane.”

“Why a crane?”

“A number of reasons, the first of which is to lift my boat out of the canal.”

Faulkner studies Lawrence for a moment then turns to the other men. “You guys, pick up their bags and water. We got Lungraun! Let’s head back to Laketon!”

Following the other two men, he leads the Lungrauns in single file back to the coach. After the other two men have boarded, he grasps Tommy and lifts him up to the step leading into the coach. One of the other men reaches down and takes Tommy by the arm to assist him up the steps.

Faulkner steps aside as Lawrence does the same for Elsie and Molly. Then Lawrence struggles aboard.

Several men leave their seats and move forward to give the family space in the back of the coach. Elsie takes a seat and slides to the window. Tommy sits beside her. Molly sits in the row behind them, slides to the window, and rests her head on the back of her seat while she closes her eyes. Lawrence joins her.

'Toot!' 'Toot!' 'Toot!'

Faulkner takes the seat across the aisle from Lawrence.

'Chug, chug.'

'Clank.' The car jerks backward.

"Tell me what happened," asks Faulkner.

Lawrence produces an exhausted smile. "A lot of people will be asking the same question. It's an experience I want to describe only once."

Then he lifts his eyebrows and with more energy queries. "What happened in Laketon?"

"We had quite a blow. A strong east wind for a solid two days. Elmer Thatcher lost his oak tree. A large branch came down on Sid Wilson's barn. Smaller tree branches and palm fronds were strewn everywhere. We helped Thatcher cut up his tree and I assigned a work crew to assist Wilson in repairing the damage to his barn."

"Get any rain?"

"Rain!" fumes Faulkner. "Boy, did it rain! It rained so hard for so long that the sand couldn't soak it up. Ended up with everything flooded. Johnson's

Hardware had six inches of water on their floor. I sent another crew out to rescue er, um, can't think of her name right now, the widow lady who lives out at the edge of town. Had to physically carry her in to the hotel."

Faulkner abruptly stops his story, raises his eyebrows, and points to Lawrence in a gesture of authority. "Tell you what. When we get to Laketon I will get word about town that you are back and are going to tell your story about what happened down at FC9. The dining room at the hotel should be big enough to hold a crowd.

Lawrence produces a small smile, leans back in his seat, and closes his eyes.

## CHAPTER 29

# DEBRIEFING

'Clang, clang.' The coach rocks enough to wake up Elsie. 'Clang, clang.' She sits up and looks out over a sea of grass standing in the late afternoon sun. Then a shanty facing the tracks drifts slowly by. A second shanty. A building with a large overhang and men working among some machinery. A street lined with houses and white picket fences. The back of a two-story brick and stucco building. Then a street lined with cars and a row of storefronts facing the tracks. The train squeaks to a stop in the Laketon town square.

Lawrence gets Faulkner's attention. "Let the work crew off first. I think we are going to be kinda slow."

“Alright you guys!” Faulkner bellows. “Hustle off the train. Be here tomorrow morning. The train leaves for FC9 on time!”

He pauses for a moment then yells louder to overcome the noise of men climbing out of their seats. “Spread the word! Lungraun is going to tell us what happened at FC9. Hotel dining room at eight o’clock tonight!”

The clamor of forty men exiting the coach dies away leaving only the Lungrauns and Stan Faulkner on board. He stands and beckons to Lawrence. “Anything more I can do to assist?”

“What time is it?”

“Fifteen to six.”

“Stores are closed, aren’t they.”

“Town shuts down at five.”

“I guess a room and a good meal would do us the best.”

Faulkner points with his thumb. “You know the way to the hotel.”

He rises and departs from the coach. Lawrence stands looking over his exhausted family. “Think you can walk another hundred feet?”

The Lungrauns struggle from the coach to the hotel reservation desk. The clerk stands erect and smiles as they approach his desk. "Welcome back to the Laketon Hotel, Mr. Lungraun. How can I help you?"

"I would like a standard room with two cots."

The clerk's smile dissolves into a slight frown. "Two cots? I have two standard rooms if you would like to spread out."

"No, a standard room with two cots will be fine. We are used to sleeping in close quarters."

"Very well, sir. I will see that Room 6 is fitted with two cots. Shall I charge the fee to your account?"

"Yes. Thanks."

Lawrence takes the key to Room 6 and they proceed down the hall. Molly mumbles. "Lawrence, we are a mess. We've been in these clothes for four days. Your shirt is split up the back from when the wind ripped it from you."

"I know," interrupts Lawrence. "All we've got are the clothes on our backs. Stores are closed. Even if we wash our clothes there won't be time enough for them to dry. The best we can do is wash up for dinner. It's already past six and there will be a crowd wanting me to say something at eight. So, let's wash up, grin and bear it, and get some food. We can all bathe and hide under sheets tonight."

Molly casts Lawrence a disparaging glance and is first to enter the room once he unlocks the door.

They arrive at the dining room with clean hands and faces. Otherwise, their remaining appearance supports their claim to four days in survival life. The host escorts them to a table away from other diners next to the wall along which rises the large mural showing water, grass, and trees against a brilliant blue sky. Molly beckons to Lawrence while pointing to a chair facing away from the mural. "I want to sit here. I've had enough of water, grass, and blue sky."

They place their orders and quietly rest while waiting for their food. When the meals arrive, they dive in, savoring the flavor of fresh-cooked food. As they finish the main course and are waiting for dessert, they notice that other tables in the dining room are filling up.

Their dessert arrives, which they eagerly devour. When they finish they notice people standing along the walls. Stan Faulkner enters the dining room and approaches Lawrence's table. "Lawrence, why don't you stand on the bench here in front of the mural so that everyone can see you?"

Lawrence rises from his seat and climbs the bench facing the crowd. Faulkner yells above the commotion and the crowd looks toward him in silence. "Listen up, folks. Let's welcome Lawrence Lungraun and his family."

Cheers and clapping.

Faulkner continues. "When we evacuated FC9 we had no way to contact Lawrence because it was at night and we had no boats. It is to our good fortune that the train we sent down to FC9 this morning picked up the Lungraun family about twenty miles south of here and brought them back."

He turns toward Lawrence and smiles. "I've asked Lawrence to tell us what happened. He has already told me that there are a number of washouts and we will need to take several loads of fill with us when we return tomorrow morning. So, Lawrence, please tell us of your experiences with the storm."

Lawrence smiles at Faulkner. "Thanks, Stan. And

thank you all for coming out. As I told Stan, my experiences with the storm are such that I want to tell about them only once."

Lawrence coughs to clear his throat. "Our adventure began early in the morning on the day of the storm. Winds were already blowing strong and I decided we would be safer if we risked the trip across the main channel to get to FC9. It was a rough crossing but we made it safely to Sutton's harbor."

Lawrence reaches down toward Molly. "Please hand me my glass of water."

After a swallow of water, he continues. "I couldn't locate Avery at his boating supply store and I became suspicious that something was amiss. I dispatched the children to the hotel, and they came back with news that the town had been evacuated. I figured that we couldn't stay at FC9 because, if things were so dangerous that all of you evacuated, the place would not be safe for us either. So I decided that we should head for the fortress."

Elsie surveys the room. Several of those standing smile and nod in approval of Lawrence's decision.

"But getting to the fortress was not easy. Seven

miles down the main channel. By now waves on the main channel were huge and the wind was so strong that running the boat at any angle to it would allow it to turn the boat. But we rigged up a way to get to the fortress by hanging the anchor on a rail and swinging the boat down parallel to the tracks."

"What direction was the wind blowing from?" interrupts someone.

"East."

Lawrence sips more water from his glass. "When we got to the fortress we thought we were safe. But the wind kept increasing and the water started rising, so we pulled the boat inside. Then the flood came. Water covered the tracks and came into the fortress. Then waves started hitting the back window. Fearing that the window might break, I lowered the hoist and ran ropes from the tie-downs on the boat to the hook on the hoist. I was trying to lift the boat above the level of the window when the window gave way. The wind blasted through the fortress and sucked out the sliding door on the trackside.

"Each time a wave hit the window, it blocked the wind and our ears popped. I was hanging onto the hoist chain for dear life in fear of being sucked out of the opening left by the sliding door…"

All over the dining room eyebrows are rising and jaws are dropping.

"…and each time a wave came in, it lifted the boat. When a wave dropped, the boat dropped with it until the tie-down ropes took hold. The boat stopped with such a jerk that Molly and the children were thrown about in the bottom of the boat. Gradually the flood rose so that the window cut off the waves and things calmed down. With some effort, Molly and the children were able to get me back into the boat.

"The flood continued to rise until we were about five feet from the ceiling. That's when we saw water coming through the wall."

"Are you saying the wind was blowing water through that wall?" queries someone with a tone of disbelief. "That wall is sixteen inches thick of solid cement."

"That's what was happening," confirms Lawrence.

Faces with mouths agape turn and look at each other. Lawrence continues. "Then part of the wall, the ceiling, and the roof were sheered off and blown away.

The hoist and all of its chains were sucked out with it. Fortunately I had unhooked the tie-down ropes or we would have gone with it."

"That's unbelievable!" exclaims a man standing along a side wall.

Lawrence looks at him and smiles. "Then the unbelievable happened. The wind was blowing at least at one hundred miles per hour, maybe much more. And suddenly it stopped. The rain ended, the clouds broke and the sun came out. We floated near the top of the fortress in the calm for a few hours. Then it clouded up again and the storm returned with the same ferocity but from the opposite direction, the west."

"That's unbelievable!" exclaims the same man.

"The storm raged with decreasing intensity for the remainder of the day and into the night. The flood receded also. The flood tore away all of the soil around the bridge, washed out roadbed, and upended hundreds of feet of track. It also washed out the foundation of the fortress causing it to tip over and submerge..."

Several men guffaw.

"...I was able to get my boat out through what

remained of the roof. Then the following day, after I cleaned out the motor, we left the fortress, set out up the canal until we ran out of fuel, then walked the rest of the way to where those of you on the train found us."

For a few moments the audience sits in stunned silence. Then several men laugh. A wave of laughter flows through the room. It becomes quiet again when Stan Faulkner stands and faces the crowd. He smiles. "Well, Lawrence, thank you for sharing your ear-popping, butt-bouncing adventure."

The room roars with laughter. Lawrence's face turns red with anger. He takes a deep breath and puffs out his chest as if to shout down the crowd. But he doesn't. The redness of his face fades and is replaced by a growing smile. As the crowd departs the room, he steps down from the bench and faces Faulkner.

The room is now empty and quiet. Faulkner turns to Lawrence and proclaims. "That was quite a story. But, one thing that bothers me is that, during all the time I have known you, you were not given to telling fanciful stories."

Without expression, Lawrence pulls a thin chain

linked to a key from around his neck. Handing the key to Faulkner, he proclaims. "Stan, this is the ignition key for my boat. When you get down toward FC9 you will find a trainload of washouts. You will find it's faster to travel by boat than by train. I suggest you take along ten cans of fuel, five to get you there and five to get you back."

With that, Molly and the children stand and join Lawrence. The four depart the dining room leaving Stan Faulkner standing alone.

CHAPTER 30

# SECRET PLAN

The first thing Elsie sees when she opens her eyes is the white ceiling of Room 6 of the Laketon Hotel. As her cot is beside the window, she reaches up and pulls back the light blue pastel curtains. The window faces the front of the hotel toward a line of train cars. The last two are flat cars, upon one of which sits a large crane. In front of them sit two gondolas filled with sand and crushed rock. Ahead of these and almost out of sight is the coach.

Men are milling about the train. Some are boarding the coach. Elsie's eyebrows rise. Lawrence is standing outside talking to Stan Faulkner.

"Sure you don't want to come with us," smiles Faulkner. "It would be an opportunity for you to personally verify your story."

"You can verify my story soon enough," smiles Lawrence. "I can't go because I have some business to take care of. I have to get Elsie off, back to Ohio, and I have to buy some clothes for my wife or I'm likely to face domestic mutiny."

Faulkner laughs.

"I can afford to take a few days off," continues Lawrence. "The main question is: 'Can I afford to buy a new lot of clothes'?"

Faulkner laughs again.

Lawrence smiles. Then his expression changes to serious. "When you get down about twenty-five miles, look for my boat at the edge of the canal. The anchor is dug in next to the tracks. Hoist the boat onto the flat car and take it with you. When you get to the washouts, you will find you can make better time in the boat."

"I had my crew pick up ten cans of fuel," Faulkner smiles. "Just in case. And I'm taking along two loads of fill."

"Not enough," replies Lawrence. "You have no idea of what you are going to face."

“Well then, it will be enough to get us started,” smiles Faulkner.

“All aboard!” sounds the distant shout from the conductor.

Faulkner turns and walks toward the train. In a few minutes Elsie watches the train cars slowly roll away.

Lawrence returns to the room carrying their canteens and food bags. Tommy is stirring and Molly is already up. Before she went to bed last night she washed all their clothes and hung them up on a rack over the bathtub to dry. She tosses clothes to Tommy and Elsie. Lawrence cajoles. “Let’s get ready for breakfast. It’s going to be a busy day.”

The four return to the dining room, which is mostly empty now that the trains have departed. Again, they are seated at the table next to the mural of water, grass, and blue sky. Shortly before they finish breakfast, the hotel supervisor, Betsy Wilson, approaches their table. “Good morning Lungrauns,” she chortles. “Lawrence, Molly, Tommy.”

Looking at Elsie, she speaks with a tone of voice to convey the impression that the girl she faces appears as a shadow of the girl she met two months ago, “And, oh yes, you must be Elsie."

Lawrence stops eating, looks up at Betsy, and touches the side of his forehead in a kind of salute. "And top of the morning to you, Betsy."

Molly nods and smiles. Elsie replies with formal courtesy, "Good morning, Missus Wilson."

Betsy continues, "My, you all look so much better today. I take it that your stay last night was peaceful."

"Oh, yes," replies Molly.

"And your breakfasts were filling?"

"Yes."

Betsy turns toward Lawrence. "Would you prefer that I add the tab to your account?"

"Yes. And, Betsy. I plan to stay tonight also. I would like you to add the additional night to my account and bring me the total of what I owe. I would like to bring my account up to date today."

Betsy smiles. "As you wish."

She turns and walks away. Molly stares at Lawrence. He wipes his face with his cloth napkin and smiles. "I want you to take the children to the store and buy them and yourself clothes sufficient to make the trip back to Ohio. Buy just enough to make the trip. We can get better things once we arrive at Canton. Add the charges to my account. Tell the owner I will come by later today and bring my account up to date."

Molly stares at Lawrence for a few moments. Then she speaks slowly and firmly. "Are you saying that you are not going back to our island?"

Lawrence leans forward and whispers. "From what we experienced at the fortress, I don't think there is an island. When we came down here, I told you that our stay would be temporary. Just long enough to make some money to gain a better life in Canton. I thought that would be until the railroad was finished. But I think the end is now."

Lawrence's eyes bore into Molly. He whispers, "Don't tell anyone that we are leaving. If anyone asks, tell them that we are just taking a vacation."

Molly leans back in her chair, closes her eyes, takes a deep breath, and smiles.

Betsy Wilson returns and presents Lawrence with a piece of paper. He studies it and asks. "This is what my balance would be tomorrow morning if I stay here tonight?"

"More than that," she proclaims. "The balance

also includes breakfast for the four of you tomorrow morning."

"Thanks, Betsy. I will be looking forward to breakfast."

As Betsy departs, Lawrence proclaims to his family. "Let's get back to the room and freshen up."

Once they have entered their room and closed the door, Lawrence continues. "Tommy and Elsie, you go with Molly to be fitted with fresh clothes. I have some business at the bank that will take a few hours and then I plan to visit Ed's Men's Store to buy some clothes for myself. After that I will go to the station and get tickets."

"Tickets!" exclaims Tommy. "Does that me we are going too? Are we going back with Elsie?"

"Yes, Tommy. I think we need to take a vacation. Furthermore, I have not had time to work with the railroad to set up escorts for Elsie, so we will have to take her ourselves. How does that sound to you?"

"Wow! Super! We can play lots of games like we did back home before we left!"

Meanwhile, Molly rummages through the food bags. "I don't think we need to worry ourselves with what remains of our food," advises Lawrence.

For a moment Molly pays him no attention. Then, from one of the bags she lifts her purse. Holding it up she proclaims. "It is ruined! The salt water ruined it!"

They depart the room and Lawrence locks the door. "Okay, I will meet you back at the hotel for lunch."

Lawrence walks along the fronts of buildings that surround the town square, acknowledging several folks who had attended his debriefing. Then he steps into the bank and walks to the teller. "May I help you?" she queries.

"Yes. I would like to visit with your illustrious bank president, Mister John Murphy."

"Please wait here."

She departs and disappears through a door behind her. She reappears in a few minutes followed by another woman. Smiling, she addresses Lawrence. "Mister Murphy would be delighted to meet with you. Missus Gibson will escort you to his office."

The woman leads Lawrence down a stained wood-paneled hallway to a door with a plaque marked 'President.' With a broad smile John Murphy stands and extends his hand to Lawrence. “Good morning, Lawrence. How can I help you? By the way, that was some story you told last night.”

“Well, John. I am going to take a vacation and I need to know how much money I have to spend.”

Murphy laughs. “I understand. It would be good for you to get out of town for awhile. It could be kind of embarrassing for you when the work crews get back.”

Lawrence nods in agreement while he laughs. “That, plus I must escort Elsie back to Ohio. Her return is already overdue.”

“So, you want to know how much money you have on deposit with us?”

“Yep.”

“Wait here. I will be back in a minute.”

Murphy rises from his chair and departs the office. In a few minutes he returns with a sheet of paper. He sits down in his swivel chair and turns toward Lawrence. “Well, Lawrence, our records show that you have with us a sum of exactly thirteen thousand, four hundred seventy-eight dollars and sixty-three cents. How much would you like to withdraw?”

"Hmmm," ponders Lawrence. "That depends on how long I will have to stay on vacation. It could be that Faulkner and his crews will return from FC9 sometime tomorrow. On the other hand, if my story is true, it may be weeks before he returns. I have a penchant to believe my story. That means I will be gone for some time, perhaps a month, while the tracks are being cleared."

Murphy becomes serious. "What do you have in mind?"

"This is what I want to do. One, I want to withdraw in cash three hundred and seventy-eight dollars and sixty-three cents. I figure I will need that much to buy new clothes and tickets, settle accounts, and house and feed a family of four on a four-day rail trip from here to Canton, Ohio. Second, I want to withdraw as a cashier's check the sum of thirteen thousand dollars."

"Wow! That is a lot of money," counsels Murphy.

"It is. My plan is to deposit the check in a bank in Canton and draw from that account as I need. Then, after Faulkner certifies that FC9 is up and running again, I can withdraw my money from the Canton bank and redeposit it here when I return."

Lawrence pauses to allow Murphy to absorb his plan. Then he continues. "Third, I will leave one hundred dollars in my account here to make sure my account remains active. The railroad owes me two weeks salary and that money will be deposited in this account."

Murphy studies the fingers on his folded hands. "Suppose you leave and the work crews return tomorrow?"

"I still have to escort Elsie back to Canton. The earliest I could return would be after ten days. You realize that I am making these decisions based on my convenience."

Murphy lowers his folded hands and looks directly at Lawrence. Then he replies. "I think I can make this work. I will authorize the teller to withdraw the cash amount you requested. When do you want the cashier's check?"

"I want to leave with the cash and the cashier's check now. I have to buy tickets and tend to the other financial business before I leave."

Murphy stands. "Follow me."

CHAPTER 30

# DEPARTURE

Shortly before noon, Lawrence, sporting a new shirt, pants, socks, and shoes, finds his way to the women's dress store. Locating the owner he queries, "Was my wife here, accompanied by two children, to buy clothes this morning?"

"Yes. She purchased a number of items for herself and the children. She said you would come by later to settle accounts."

"That is why I am here," smiles Lawrence.

When Lawrence departs the women's store, it is midday so he proceeds to the hotel to meet his family for lunch. He finds them seated at a table near the middle of the dining room amid other diners. "Wow! You and Elsie look different. If I hadn't recognized

Tommy I would have missed you. And what's this? A purse?"

Molly lifts her new purse from her lap and opens it. She withdraws her prized possession, her mother's pearl necklace. She places the necklace back into the purse. Smiling broadly, she replies. "Someone has to carry your toothbrush. How did it go for you?"

"I wasn't sure Murphy would be willing to release that much money at once. I cleared all of my accounts and…."

Lawrence points toward his chest. "…got some new clothes."

He rubs his hand along his face. "This afternoon, I need to visit the barber and secure tickets for tomorrow's train to Tampa."

Molly smiles. "Then so far so good. This afternoon Elsie and I are going to visit the hairdresser. Why don't you take Tommy along with you to the barber? He could gain some 'man' experience, and besides, he could do with a fresh haircut."

Lawrence beckons to Tommy. "Okay son, let's go."

After a long wait for two chairs to open simultaneously, Lawrence and Tommy take their seats.

Pointing to Tommy, Lawrence commands. Haircut for my son. Shave and a haircut for me."

Since it is part of the job description for barbers to be conversational, Lawrence's barber begins. "Shave and a haircut. You're not trying to change your appearance are you?"

"Going to take a vacation."

"Given the tale you told yesterday, I'd take a vacation too."

Lawrence says nothing. Then Tommy's barber adds. "I've heard of sunny skies with calm winds going to stormy with one hundred mile per hour winds. Had storms like that in Kansas. But I've never heard of stormy with one hundred mile per hour winds going to sunny and calm. Are you sure you didn't get your story backwards?"

"No way!" interrupts Tommy. "It happened just the way my dad said it happened!"

The barbers finish their haircuts in silence.

Lawrence and Tommy walk side by side to the train station. As they approach the ticket window the teller stands at attention. "Mister Lungraun, where are you going?"

"I need four tickets for tomorrow morning's train to Tampa."

"Four tickets?"

"Yep. I'm taking a vacation."

The man laughs. "From what I hear, it would seem to be a good time for you to take a vacation."

Lawrence smiles as he lays down money sufficient to pay for the tickets. "Yes. It's a very good time for me to take a vacation."

"Well, you and your son certainly look like travelers."

'Stamp.' 'Stamp.' 'Stamp.' 'Stamp.'

"Here are your tickets. Four coach seats to Tampa. Have a good trip."

Lawrence and Tommy return to their hotel room to join Molly and Elsie. Seeing Molly, Lawrence exclaims. "Wow! You look beautiful!"

"It's been a long time since I've been to a hairdresser."

"Why don't we go down to dinner now so we have time for a good night's rest? The train leaves at eight o'clock in the morning."

'Knock, knock, knock!' 'Knock, knock, knock!' "Mister Lungraun? Lawrence Lungraun? It's six o'clock."

"Thank you."

By six-thirty the Lungrauns are in the dining room for breakfast. The room is crowded but there are still a number of empty tables. "Eat up!" commands Molly. "I've put some snacks in my purse, but, it's still going to be a long ride."

As they finish, Betsy Wilson approaches their table. "I take it everything is satisfactory," she smiles. "Indeed so," replies Lawrence as he reaches into his pocket. He extracts a piece of paper and hands it to Betsy. "I presume the bottom line is still correct."

She nods. Lawrence hands her cash to cover the total. She returns and gives the bill to Lawrence. Below the total is written 'Paid in full.'

Betsy smiles again. "Y'all have a good and safe vacation. And, if I don't see you again, may all of you be blessed."

Then she turns toward Elsie. "Goodbye, Elsie."

Elsie nods. "Goodbye, Missus Wilson."

After breakfast they walk slowly from the hotel

into the town square. Standing there is the Tampa train. They each carry a small travel bag containing something to do or read to occupy one's time during the long train ride.

Elsie looks at a small column of steam and smoke rising from the locomotive. Behind the tender is the baggage car followed by five box cars. At the end sits the passenger coach. The conductor, whom Elsie doesn't recognize, stands by a step near the rear of the car. A small group of perhaps ten passengers, all men, mills about. The Lungrauns stand at the edge of the group.

After awhile the conductor withdraws his pocket watch and looks at the time. He surveys his crowd and beckons the Lungrauns to come forward. "Okay everybody. It's time to board. I have a family over here. Stand back and let the ladies board first."

Elsie stands at the front of the line. The conductor assists her up the steps into the coach. Then it's Molly's turn. Elsie enters the coach, finds her old seat and slides to the window. Molly slides to the window in the seat behind her. Then Tommy takes his seat next to Elsie and Lawrence sits behind him.

"All aboard."

The remaining passengers take their seats.

After a few minutes there is a slight jerk and Elsie notices movement outside. The storefronts across the town square are moving slowly past her. Then the back of a two-story brick and stucco building, a street lined with white picket fences, and a building with a long overhanging roof where there are men working among some machinery glide past. These are followed by several shanties and then grass. Laketon is left behind.

'Clang, clang.' The coach rocks slightly. 'Clang, clang.' Looking out the window Elsie watches the locomotive come into view as the train slowly rounds a sharp curve. 'Clang, clang.' 'Clang, clang.' They pass over a siding, the track straightens, and they are headed west.

The familiar sea of grass welcomes Elsie. After a while she grows bored, turns to the travel bag in the seat next to her, and extracts a book and a pen. She opens the book and begins to write.

*Dear Diary. Today is the 10th of August of 1927. I am on the train, the train with the little engine, on my way to Tampa. Lawrence, Molly, and Tommy Lungraun are with me. This day begins my four-day trip from Laketon, Florida, to Canton, Ohio. My vacation at Lungraun's Island is over. I am amazed that I remember so little. Even the storm. Several days ago when I closed my eyes, memories of the storm came back in terrifyingly vivid color. Even when Uncle Lawrence told of our adventures after our return to Laketon I cringed at times. Now most of the memories have become black and white. I wonder what I will remember tomorrow.*

*I wonder what happened to my first diary. Will I ever see it again? Maybe someday someone will find it and return it to me.*

Elsie lowers her pen as she rereads her entry. Then, closing the book, she places it and her pen back into the small travel bag sitting next to her on the weathered leather seat. She leans toward the open window and loses herself in the sea of grass passing by.

After awhile Tommy notices her. Sliding next to her he queries. "Elsie, what to you see?"

She turns slightly to see Tommy out of the corner of her eye and smiles.

"Gazelles."

# EPILOGUE

Stan Faulkner and his work crews make good time as their train chugs south from Laketon toward FC9. After they have gone about twenty-five miles, the locomotive slows and brakes squeal as it stops next to a boat anchor located by the rails. The crew assists the engineer to move the train so that the crane is positioned directly opposite Lawrence's boat. Then the boat is lifted from the canal and placed on the flatcar behind the crane.

They make good time for the next forty-five minutes. Then the locomotive slows to a stop once again. The engineer sees a discoloration in the roadbed under the tracks.

It is a minor washout and, on Faulkner's orders, is quickly filled by work crews.

Twenty minutes later the train stops again. This time the washout is larger and deeper. As crews work to repair the roadbed, Faulkner selects two men and orders them to walk the tracks for about a mile and report back. In the meantime, he happens to look at the grass that lines the opposite side of the canal. The grass is bent over and broken.

The two men return with a grim report. The farther they walked the more washouts they saw. Finally, they approached a washout so large that the two loads of fill would not be enough to repair it.

Faulkner sets the crews to work repairing the washouts as best they can. Meanwhile he orders Lawrence's boat to be unloaded and set in the canal. He and five other men load the boat with food, water, and fuel and begin exploration of the storm damage further down the tracks.

Eventually they come to areas where sections of track are upended and where there are more sections of rail totally washed out than there is track that remains. Then they come to the bridge over the main channel, the bridge that Lawrence had described as standing naked on its supports, all the surrounding roadbed having been washed away.

They pull ashore and stand looking toward the mostly submerged fortress. No one speaks. They all now know that Lawrence Lungraun was telling the truth.

They reboard the boat and continue south, searching for the spur that runs to FC9. After passing several sections of submerged track, they locate the spur and turn west. They know that FC9 is seven miles distant from their location.

They follow the tracks for about a mile until the tracks disappear beneath the waves. Finally, after they have gone an estimated additional six miles, they stop.

There are no mangrove trees; there are no buildings; there is no grass; there is no sand! Just water as far as the eye can see.

Fletcher Camp Nine has vanished!

# ACKNOWLEDGEMENTS

I am grateful to my wife, Sue, for her critical reviews of the manuscript.

I am also indebted to Mr. Jack McNeil (professional graphic artist) for rendering the manuscript into book format and creating the cover graphics.

# BOOKS BY CLIFTON WELSH
# (AVAILABLE ON AMAZON)

## UNDER THE RADAR
## THE PRINCE RETURNS
## THE BABYLON AFFAIR
## BE THOU MY VISION
## MCCLEAVER

Made in the USA
Columbia, SC
06 December 2023

27918690R00139